I0623379

THROUGH A
GLASS
DARKLY

TISHIA DOBSON

Rainmaker Publishing

First published by Rainmaker Publishing 2025
Savannah, GA 31421
www.timetogetpublished.com
Copyright © 2025 by Tishia Dobson

Paperback ISBN: 978-1-961351-35-6
First Edition

Cover design by Lauria
Interior customized and prepared by Rainmaker Publishing

In Memory Of

Tishia "Tish" Mishe Chevez Dobson
January 11, 1969 – February 8, 2023

A gifted storyteller, devoted teacher, and woman of unwavering faith,
whose imagination and spirit live on through the words on these pages.

For Tish
From Stanton, Stanton Jr., and Bhrea

This book is more than a story—it is a reflection of your heart, your faith, and the wonder that lived in your imagination. We watched you breathe life into these pages with the same love, patience, and creativity you brought to everything you touched.

You taught us how to live with purpose, how to lead with kindness, and how to stay grounded in our faith. You made room for magic in the everyday—and now that magic will live on in the hands of every reader.

We miss you deeply, but we carry your light forward.

This is for you, always.

"We do not always recognize the shape of grace when it first arrives—but even in shadow, the light waits to be claimed."

— T.D.

CONTENTS

DEDICATION

All of my words are first dedicated to my Lord and Savior, Jesus Christ. Without His loving kindness, without His mercy, without His stabilizing hand, I would not have been able to accomplish the first of many dreams. Next, I dedicate this work to my family: my loving and supportive husband, Stan Sr., and my very own Noble and Lark, my children Stanton and Bhrea. I am so blessed to have you all in my life. Thank you for your encouragement and your unconditional love. I love you so much. I also thank my mother, Gloria, who has always encouraged me to follow my dreams and Momma Jackie who has heartened me to do the same. This dedication would not be complete without special acknowledgement of Josephine who never allowed me to give up on my dream and has been with me at every stage of my novel's development and Kim who gave me the courage to complete it. I also dedicate this work to the women of Savannah Technical College: your love, guidance, and encouragement have bolstered me throughout this process. Finally, I dedicate this work to every woman in the spirit of mothering who has "mothered" me along the way either by kind deed or word, nurturing me to complete this work and to become the woman I am destined to be.

To all of my "Village", I offer heartfelt and humbling thanks.

Tish

P.S. My last dedication is to all those who suffer from chronic illness, whether it is sickle cell disease or cancer or mental illness. Your disease is not the full sum of who you are. Laughter and joy and fulfillment and passion cannot be measured in pain. In fact, it is pain that makes these moments in life that much more worthwhile and priceless. And while I may suffer from sickle cell, I find that being a wife, mother, sister, daughter, aunt, friend, and teacher a truer statement of who I am. Having a chronic illness does not define me. What I am able to accomplish between hospital visits and pain episodes does. Learning to follow my passions and seek life outside of pain makes my life full of love, rich and full.

AESTHETIC STATEMENT

"Fantasy: A Not-So-New Metaphor for Faith"

The type of work I wish to create is a spiritual fantasy that speaks to a lost generation of youth suffering spiritual disconnect, emotional distance, and family separation. I had hoped that the works of Christian authors C.S. Lewis and J.R.R. Tolkien and other writers with similar themes would largely influence the young adult fantasy I'm trying to create. However, I contend that this current generation is not one who will be reached through the didactic messages and themes of Lewis and Tolkien. Nor is this generation one who will be impacted by fiction that draws sharp and rigid lines between good and evil or black and white so severely. I want my fiction to expand on these edifying and moralizing messages; rather, I want my fiction to touch children who need more realistic and authentic messages that will affect them wherever they are on their "moral compass" and leave them with an arresting message that will change their lives for the better. I want a message that extends beyond the "finger pointing" and "ought to haves" that would have worked in my day.

In the beginning pages of *The Magician's Nephew*, C.S. Lewis takes the adolescent reader into a world where although the protagonists suffer from their own personal issues, moral obligations and responsibility are firmly in tact:

"And if your father was away in India, -- and you had to come and live with an Aunt and Uncle who is mad (who would like that!) – and if the reason was that they were looking after your Mother – and if your Mother was ill and was going to—going to die." Then his face went the wrong sort of shape as it does when you're trying to hold back tears.

"I didn't know," said Polly humbly. And then, because she hardly knew what to say, and also to turn Digory's mind to cheerful subjects, she asked, "Is Mr. Ketterly really mad?" (Lewis 12).

In Lewis's novel, while Digory struggles with his father's deployment to India and his mother's declining health, the reader is made to realize that his father having to fight in a war is an acceptable, given responsibility if not a right. Lewis's novel reflects a society that believes that when someone in the family suffers, other family members step in to shoulder the obligations of the affected member, thus the mother's care and that of her son's. Again, these responsibilities, these "ought-to's", are as understandable, are as accepted, and are as natural as Polly's attempt to steer Digory's mind away from troubling thoughts of his mother's death. After all, in Lewis's didactic text, isn't that what one *ought* to do? Responsibility and obligation are givens in Lewis's world but not necessarily in today's, where the welfare system is rife with abandoned children in foster homes, and family members do not feel obligated to assume their sibling's duties as their own.

In this current world, families are fractured, and community is a word that connotes no common bonds between members. The distinctions between right and wrong are less rigid and not as severe in today's society, and the young may not always choose the "right thing" to, especially when she doesn't feel as secure and safe in such a system. In such a society, what do young adults look to for direction?

I want my novel series *Through a Glass Darkly* to address a generation of young persons who are complex mixtures of both shadow and light. Because I want to address issues of chronic illness, depression, mental illness, and other personal demons, I look to authors such as Octavia Butler whose characters aren't "cookie cutter" creations as in *Wild Seed* or as in Orson Scott Card's *Song Master.* These books show that in spite of hardship, the human spirit can still triumph. I want to use authors like Orson Scott Card or even the splendor of the musical *The Whiz* to show that there can be truth and beauty even in suffering.

I also look to Sherilyn Kenyon's *Acheron,* Octavia Butler's *Wild Seed,* and fictions by great writers such as Flannery O'Connor and Jane Yolen because like these writers, I desire to create stories that use fantasy to make changes in otherwise gruesome settings and backgrounds. It is not my intent to mislead our young readers with illusions of fairy tales, but rather in the tradition of old story tellers, offer hope from the characters that I craft and the stories that I create. My characters must deal with real loss, with the overwhelming illness of sickle cell disease (named "chee-wee-chee-wee" by ancient African traditions to imitate the chewing and gnawing nature of the crisis pain), and with death and overcome these hardships with hope and the "fantasy" of faith. However, I don't want to limit faith to mere fantasy but rather make faith more real to today's adolescent through the fantastical. Craft instructs by Orson Scott Card, *How to Write Science Fiction and Fantasy,* and Ursula LeGuinn quoted in *The Wand in the Word* provide practical guidance for creating such themes in fantasy. Finally, I am inspired by James N. Frey's instructional text on writing fiction. Gloria Naylor's *Mamma Day* is also very enlightening for the wonder and magic she weaves in her stories. It is my dream to create a work that inspires a generation like *The Whiz* did for its viewers. I want to give my readers a voice for the hardships they encounter in their generation and some strategies such as the "fantasy" of faith to overcome them.

My novel uses many of the themes and devices used in the stories I've listed. I want it to have a spiritual influence like Tolkien and Lewis, but rather than clobbering my reader over the head with didactic messages, as mentioned above, I want to create a metaphor for fantasy, faith, that provides young people with a real tool for confronting real demons. I want my fiction to have the depth and splendor found in the works of Octavia Butler, Neil Gaiman, Orson Scott Card, Sherilynn Kenyon, Jane Yolen, and Gloria Naylor. Besides, I will need something more than mere wand waving and hocus pocus to help my readers deal with demons they must face each and every day: chronic illness like sickle cell disease, mental illness, mental and physical abuse, poverty, bullying, low self-esteem, and confusion and identity issues. In Through a Glass Darkly, the veil has been lifted, and the main character Noble is able to discern that all of these demons simply wear the guise of "issues" that my characters must learn to combat and overcome. My protagonists are like the teens today who live in a new world; they must simply learn that the world they call "real" is larger and more frightening than they've been taught to believe. Their only chance for survival is the Light. I hope my aims live up to my extremely high expectations, for it is a fantasy I'm trying to create with moral impact and significance for adolescents today.

READING LIST

Butler, Octavia. *Wild Seed*. New York, New York: Warner Books, 1980. Print.

Card, Orson Scott. *Songmaster.* New York, New York: Tom Doherty and Associates, LLC, 1978. Print.

Card, Orson Scott. *How to Write Science Fiction and Fantasy.* Cincinatti, Ohio: Writer's Digest Books, 2001. Print.

Frey, James N. *The Key: How to Write Damn Good Fiction Using the Power of Myth.* New York, New York: St. Martin's Press, 2000. Print.

Gaiman, Neil. *Anansi Boys*. New York, New York: Harper Collins, 2005. Print.

Kenyon, Sherilynn. *Acheron*. New York, New York: St. Martin's Press, 2008. Print.

Lewis, C.S. *The Magician's Nephew*. New York, New York: Harper Collins, 1955. 12. Print.

Naylor, Gloria. *Mama Day*. New York, New York: Random House, Inc., 1988. Print.

Tolkien, J.R.R. *The Hobbit*. 50th Anniversary Authoritative Revised. New York, New York: Houghton Mifflin, 1988. Print.

Yolen, Jane. *The Wand in the Word*. Ed. Leonard S. Marcus. First edition. Candlewick Press, 2006. Print.

PROLOGUE

THE ICE CREAM MAN

Lightning ripped a ragged gash across the heavens. No rain followed. At 10:38 pm, on an unusually balmy October evening, a white ice cream truck with a claw in the form of a letter D, a cage made out of bones, and a skull with its mouth frozen agape in fear, rounded the corner of the main road of Salvation, Georgia and ambled for Juniper Avenue, the street that led to the housing projects of Warren Homes and Fraiser Complex. To the accidental glance, a child's unassuming gaze, the alley cat or stray dog's wary notice, the ice cream truck did not seem to move on wheels at all, but rather loped along at a slow predator's gait. Toddlers ran for the comfort of their mothers' arms. Alley cats hissed, their ears flattened back, and the few stray dogs yelped and whined as they ran for cover.

Tuesday evening slumbered on, quiet yet dangerous. Most of the project residents were indoors. Those who had endured the long day partied, drank, or slept away the harsh inequities of their lives. Others escaped into drugs or fighting. Even the neighborhood sots, who loitered around the evening street lights most nights, drank their cheap wine from inside their homes. And usually, an ice cream truck with a skull and claws would have been a peculiar sight indeed, at the dead end of fall, approaching an unseasonably cold and rough winter. Most children would have been inside, but on this particular evening, a rainless night of vengeful lightning and unseasonably, warm breezes, little Keisha

Williams, four years old in multi-colored, beaded braids, wandered the street just outside her apartment, as her mother played Spades and drank beer down the hall with friends.

"Take that, suckers!" Keisha's mother Brenda slapped a ten of spades on the table. "I knew y'all jokers were out of clubs!" She yanked a sagging, red bra strap back onto her shoulder, a certain "tell" to the other players that she felt a winning streak if they were sober enough to have noticed. They didn't.

"And that!" Brenda said slapping down a seven of spades.

Keisha skipped on, just noticing the eerie glow of the peculiar signs and symbols that covered the ancient ice cream truck. As Keisha stared at the approaching truck, the driver of the vehicle, hidden from view by impenetrable, pitch windows, turned on the music.

"That too!" Brenda said slapping down another spade. She sipped on her beer and smiled as the other card players slapped down their cards in disappointing grunts.

At once, Keisha noticed that the music, more of a dangerous tinkling and peculiar chiming, was not the normal tune that blared from the ice cream truck on a summer day. But, Keisha was hungry. Her mother had given her a candy bar and a Co-cola, her only supper, before sauntering off to her card game. Keisha's stomach grumbled and growled as she remembered the cold space ship pops that numbed her lips and gums with strawberry sweetness and the ice cream sandwiches whose creamy middles always melted away before she munched the chocolate wafers that her Uncle Tyrone had bought her last summer.

"You might as well give 'em up!" Brenda said, pulling up her bra strap again. "Mm-hmmm, that's right." She smiled as she played her last three winning cards, grinning at the other players' grunts and frowns.

Keisha didn't have any money, but the ice cream truck now less than ten feet from the unattended and lonely child beckoned. If Keisha had paid attention, she would have seen that the funny symbols on the truck had changed to images of sweet treats, of ice pops, and fudge-cycles.

She would have detected the unearthly smell of singe and sulfur and the low growl of a hell hound. She would have noticed that the ice cream man who leered from pitch windows did not have human hands at all but scaly, four-fingered claws. The ice cream man pulled up directly in front of Keisha, cornering her in a dark alley. Mesmerized by the music, her hunger, and the memory of the chocolate chip ice cream sandwich, Keisha skipped forward. Her little feet found the rhythm of the haunting, lilting tune, and her multi-colored, beaded braids clicked and jingled.

She did not notice as two hell hounds, Glut and Glomit, with stretched, grotesque faces and the bodies of monstrous hounds, too hideous to be friendly dogs, appeared behind her, their mouths drooling, their eyes, glowing red orbs, and what would have been nostrils, mere slits in a ghoulish, inhuman face. She didn't discover until it was too late that the ice cream driver was really not a man at all but a grotesque and ill formed demon with rows of sharp, uneven teeth and scaly, monstrous hands. Keisha screamed and turned to run away. The hell hounds cornered her, snapping at her feet, and leered at her flowing tears and feeble cries.

"Mommy!" Little Keisha cried.

The demon laughed a dry, voiceless laugh. He inhaled deeply, savoring the aroma of her panic and fear.

In the shadows, unseen by the hell-hounds and The Beast, a feint, glimmering light floated towards the whimpering girl. It glimmered closer until finally it hovered in the air above her. The light grew a little brighter, shimmering on top of her. Finally, it enveloped her, bathing her in its warm glow. From the midst of the light, a soft, gentle voice hummed. Entranced, Keisha stopped sobbing. The humming grew louder and then paused.

"This little light of mine.... I'm gonna' let it shine...

This little light of mine... I'm gonna' let it shine...

This little light of mine... I'm gonna' let it shine...

Let it shine, let it shine, let it shine..." the gentle voice sang.

Keisha hiccupped in her hysteria, trying to focus on the gentle voice in spite of the gaping jaws that loomed over her. Even in her panic, she noticed that both the hounds and The Beast were frozen and had not advanced any closer.

"Don't be afraid, Keisha. I've come to help you," the gentle voice beckoned. Keisha hiccupped less, her crying altogether stopped.

"Can you remember this song?" the voice asked.

Keisha nodded her head yes. She remembered the songs her Grammy sang as the choir sang loudly in church, the few times her mother allowed her to visit. Lying on her Grammy's song-filled chest, as she rocked and hugged her, Keisha felt warm, loved, and safe. Keisha nodded again.

"I'm going to cover you with *grace*. To us, it looks like sparkling mist." While the voice spoke, a gentle mist of light and dew enveloped Keisha, calmed her.

"They won't be able to see it, and while it covers you, they won't be able to touch you. This will protect you until the Lightbearer comes. All you have to do is hope. Keep hope until the Lightbearer comes. You will know him by his courage, and his strength, but most of all, you will know him by the light he carries. It's all around him. It's within him. It is him. Can you do that?"

Keisha nodded and sniffled, clutching a fold of the *grace* to her cheek. It felt like the soft blanket she used to fall asleep most nights. It was both cool and warm, and it soothed her in this terrifying environment.

"Keep humming this song, Keisha. They will take you, but they can't touch you. Keep the song alive. Keep hope of his coming alive, and he will come. He will come to save you and all the others ..." The voice became softer and the glowing light lifted, but the blanket of *grace* remained.

"Be brave!" it called softly. "The Lightbearer comes."

The glimmering light paled and then dissolved. All but the humming remained. Keisha gathered the *grace*, a gossamer cloak of stars blinking on the surface of the night, closer around her shoulders and under her chin.

The hounds and The Beast resumed their advance, oblivious to the cloak or the gentle, humming voice. Keisha raised her chin in brave defiance. The Beast gathered the darkness around her like a coarse, black sack, and carried Keisha within. The hounds snapped at the other-worldly sack, and Keisha hummed inside until the space in the world that was once Keisha was no more. The lightning once again slashed across the sky. At long last, thunder answered in a low rumble and was silent.

Brenda quickly raked in her winnings and hurriedly stuffed them in her bra. She would count them later. Experience had taught her that counting winnings in front of a disgruntled, losing group was suicide.

"Next time Tuesday night," Brenda said. She'd give Lynnette her cut later. They had rigged the deck earlier, causing her unlikely win. They wouldn't be able to keep up the deception much longer. Even drunken players became suspicious. Brenda grabbed her purse and quit the room. She had a sudden, compelling thought to check on Keisha to make sure wasn't in danger, to make sure she was alright. She felt her baby's intense fear and heard her cries. But the thought quickly vanished. She pulled out a five dollar bill from her bra and hurried to corner liquor store before it closed. Besides, Keisha would sleep through the night. She always did. Brenda thought to visit her boyfriend on the second floor. He would certainly be waiting up for her. She pulled another five out of her bra.

"Better make it a six pack," she said. Brenda hurried down the street to the liquor store. An ice cream truck drove by and halted in front of her. The truck made her fearful in ways she couldn't explain.

"What 'chu looking at?" Brenda yelled. "I didn't ask for no ice cream!" She stared at the black windows. Fear and panic crept inside her. She hurried along.

The Beast inside the ice cream truck snickered. He watched Brenda's retreating figure in the rear view mirror. With cold, calculating eyes he watched as she glanced over her shoulder at him often, putting as much distance as she could between her and the truck. He laughed again, dry and voiceless and drove on.

1

Dreams, Warnings, and First Day Jitters

Noble gasped in his sleep. He was having the same terrifying nightmare. The cold, billowing clouds descended upon him. In their murky depths he heard the familiar howls of anguish, the weeping, the gnashing and gnawing. He struggled to hear whimpering and the heavy breathing of someone being chased, of someone … familiar. The image of a screaming, tear-stained, little girl with clicking braids flashed in his mind. She called out to her mother, but dogs, unlike any dogs he'd ever seen, closed in on her. Within a muted space of darkness, he heard her muffled tone …. humming. *A nursery rhyme? No. A gospel tune?* Noble couldn't say for sure. What he did recognize was the same inhuman voice that called out to him in nightmares before. The voice reminded him of dead leaves scuttling around in the wind's mischief, taunting him, tormenting him. Without seeing, he never needed to see to know they were there, he knew cold, damp, dead things lurked within.

The voice called out to him. Noble cringed.

"I come for you!" it hissed. "I come for you and all you hold dear, Lighted One. I snatch another innocent from your world, and I come for you. Once I have the Blood of Seven, no one will be able to defeat me. Not the Light. Not the Wise Ones. And not you. Bow to me. Surrender to the Darkness while you still can. Your death will be quick. Make no mistake. I will kill you. I will destroy you and all that you hold dear, Son of Light."

A cacophony of angry, confused howls, anguished shrieks and mad, despairing laughter deafened his ears. And as always, Noble heard the horrible sound of gnawing and chewing, as if a million, sinister mouths feasted on tender, exposed flesh. In the cloud's dark center, he noticed a glittering light. It winked at him beneath shadows. In spite of a paralyzing fear, he made for the light's feint glimmer. Sweat clung to the narrow space between his shoulder blades and slicked icy behind his neck. The darkness, sensing his escape, swirled and rumbled. Noble heard the dry, voiceless laugh that was pure evil. He felt sharp pain rip his thigh and left arm. Wave upon wave of terror and despair engulfed him as the dark cloud bore down on him, the mouths too close now, making escape nearly impossible. A cold, clammy hand, grey and rotting, ascended from the mire and muck and reached out through the shadows. Just as Noble broke for the light, the rotting arm grabbed him by the throat and stroked his cheek.

"The Blood of Seven!" the voice yelled. Noble opened his mouth to a silent scream.

Noble sat up. His trembling, goose-bumped back made a ninety degree angle with his rumpled bed. He wiped the cold sweat from his brow and glanced over at his alarm clock; the red numerals glared 6:00 am. There was no use trying to go back to sleep. Searing panic in his chest always made sleep impossible.

He didn't know how, but he knew, no felt, that this day was going to be incredibly horrible. More horrible than its normal routine crumminess. Yes, he was probably going to be pummeled by Ray Capers and his cronies. Yes, he would probably embarrass himself in some excruciatingly painful way, like the time he was in such a rush to get to Public School 119 that he forgot to put on his navy, uniform pants and showed up in his orange plaid boxers in front of his secret crush Melody Stevens. And yes, he was going to be tormented and jeered by his peers. Ninth grade was no different than seventh or eighth, except that this year, to add insult to injury, his mother would be his Advanced Comp/Lit. Teacher.

Resigning himself for the worst, he reached over to the nightstand on the other side of his bed and shut off the alarm clock before it sounded. The red numerals now glared 6:03. He swung both legs over the edge of the bed and willed himself up. Yawning and scratching the back of his head, he stumbled in the darkness to the bathroom he and his younger sister Lark shared. The pre-dawn darkness made ghostly shapes of the furniture as he nearly tripped over a stray basketball. He counted himself lucky to have beaten her there before her daily metamorphosis.

He switched on the bathroom light and purposely ignored the scattering of inky, undefined, creepiness that hovered just beyond his peripheral vision. This was not the time to focus on the fact that he probably was insane. Who else could dream such violent dreams night after night and see the unexplainable by day? He focused on his image in the mirror instead. His reflection gazed back at him: Wide hazel eyes framed by thick, dark lashes, his peanut-butter complexion, a curious mix of his father's bronze skin and his mother's glowing, butter color. His mouth, full lips like his mother's, formed a reassuring smile. It was one he was sure he did not make. He ignored his smiling reflection and stepped into the shower. He braced himself for the icy blast before the water at last turned warm. The massaging warmth melted away his jitters. He worked the soap and heated water into frothy suds. As the water and soap enveloped his body, he jumped at biting stings in his thigh and left arm. He brushed the soap and water from his eye and bent forward to examine the cause of the sting. Blood swirled above an open wound in his thigh. Noble dabbed at it with his wash cloth. Beneath the cloth lay ragged torn skin; Noble bent his face closer. It was a bite mark. He raised his left arm for inspection and found its twin, another bite. A brisk rapping rattled the door, interrupting his inspection. He jumped at the sound and pulled back the shower curtain.

"Open up, Nobby!" his sister Lark yelled. "We don't have all day!"

Noble flinched, startled again by his sister's intrusion. He snatched his blue towel from the rack, barely enveloped his waist in its plush, terry softness, and squeezed toothpaste on his Sponge Bob toothbrush before his sister's incessant pounding annoyed him again. He concentrated on small, chary circles inside and outside the gum line.

"Wait your turn, Phony!" he yelled through a mouthful of toothpaste.

Nettled by his nickname of her, Lark picked open the lock on the door with a hair pin and intruded on his grooming.

"Hey! What the Corn Fritter?" he screamed, clutching the towel around his narrow frame. "What if I was using the john or ..."

"Scratching your butt or picking your nose?" she interrupted. "Don't worry. Your dirty, little secrets are safe with me."

"You make me sick," he said spitting into the sink. He threw the toothpaste tube at her with vengeful aim hoping to clip her or at least cause a minor Winter-fresh stain on her favorite pink robe, but she caught it deftly in her hand and floated past him into the bathroom.

"Me too, Corn Fritters," Lark answered. "Do me a favor and don't say that at school. After all, I do have a reputation to protect." Her wavy, thick, brown hair was gathered in hair rollers, and hazel eyes stared back at him behind a peculiar green mud mask.

"What was this, an alien invasion?" Noble asked.

Lark stuck out his tongue in response, shifting her bulge of cosmetic sundries stuffed in a matching pink bag under the arm of her pink bathrobe. She slammed the door after him.

"I don't know why you insist on buying all that face paint when you know you can't wear it," Noble yelled at the closed door.

In his room, with the door closed and his bedroom light and desk lamp glaring for extra visibility, Noble examined the bites. Somehow the ragged torn skin had mended and knitted into visible scars, but the scars were without question bites. He searched his room for evidence of a small rat or animal. He found none.

Noble's rational mind excused away what he knew to be true: that rats did not make those bites. The monstrous mouths in his dream did, but he would not permit another freaky thought in his life of creepy occurrences to ruin his first day of school.

The clock now glared 6:26 a.m., and Noble knew he would have to hustle if he wanted to eat breakfast and make the 6:45 a.m. bus. He could hear his mother's bustling downstairs, and that made him hurry. As he dressed, his stomach bubbled and his pulse raced. The feeling of dread he had awakened to this morning still clung to him. He felt a curious stirring of excitement in his stomach, like something significant, life changing, or maybe even dangerous was going to happen today.

"Breakfast's on the table!" his mother beckoned, yelling up the stairs. The aroma of maple sausages, oatmeal, and coffee wafted upstairs.

Later at the breakfast table, he noticed his mother Genesis fully dressed in her beginning-of-the-year, no-nonsense, grey, pinstriped suit. She stirred a pot of oatmeal with half of her sandy-red hair in curlers and the other half cascading down her shoulders. He knew before breakfast was over, she would clean the breakfast dishes, wash and fold a load of clothes, take out the rest of her rollers, confine her hair to her signature French roll and blot on her only makeup, a wine or copper-colored lipstick that complimented her glowing, golden skin. She never wanted her appearance to detract from teaching her students, but in spite of her careful preparations, she was a woman of striking beauty.

"Good morning, Nobby," she crooned. He loved his mother's rich alto voice and sprinkling of freckles across her button nose and cheeks. But these attributes did nothing to endear her to him as his Comp/Lit and homeroom teacher this year.

"Morning," he groaned.

Her eyes squinted at him and she wrinkled her freckled nose in concentration. She ladled steaming oatmeal in his bowl and sprinkled it with brown sugar, butter, raisins, and cinnamon.

"Are you feeling okay?" she asked as she placed the steaming bowl in front of him at his place at the table. She placed a hand upon his forehead. "Is it first day of school jitters?" she asked. Noble noticed his mother's radar worked overtime this morning. He felt the weight of her penetrating stare. He hunkered down to her inspection.

No, it's I don't want my mom to be my teacher jitters, he wanted to say but instead muttered, "No, Ma'am, I'm okay." He knew he was under his mother's scrutiny, and he pretended to be more interested in his breakfast and the décor of the kitchen than any touchy talk of fears and feelings. He felt them, of course, but he didn't want to admit them or tread into territory in which he never felt comfortable: confiding to his mother. *What was next? Talk of "normal" male hormones and peculiar, naughty dreams? Yeach! No thank you.* So he surveyed the walls of the kitchen instead.

The kitchen was his favorite room in their house on Azalea Lane. It was decorated in a rich, golden color with accents of sunflowers, his mother's favorite bloom, on every wall. Herbs grew in a hodge-podge assortment of pots in the window, and a framed kitchen blessing, a sign that hung over their antique gas stove, read: *Love covers a multitude of sins.* It was the only room in the house that hadn't changed after his father's disappearance in the Middle East four months ago. All the other rooms in their home had retained their antiquated yet stately character, littered with old fashioned mahogany and cherry furniture. Some rooms had grown quite drafty, dark, and dismal. An unspoken sadness settled in during his father's absence and blanketed the house like a heavy cloak.

"Are you sure?" Genesis pressed further. "Because if you're not feeling well, you don't have to go to school today." She placed her lips to his forehead, a gesture she hadn't shown since he was six. As a child, the gesture comforted Noble as his mother checked his temperature. At fourteen, he found it smothering.

Noble dropped the four hot link sausages he was attempting to stuff into his mouth. They tumbled over each other on his plate.

"Are *you* okay?" he asked. His mother had never allowed him to miss a day of school without a darned good reason, bordering death, imminent injury, or some other calamity.

"It's just ..." she said. "Well, there's been a series of kidnappings lately. And we don't know who's doing it or why. .... It's nothing I'm sure. I don't want to worry you unnecessarily, but just be careful, okay?"

She smiled at him and rubbed her hip absently with one hand as she placed the pot of oatmeal back on the stove with the other and then turned down the heat. It was Noble's turn to frown. Noble's mother had chee-wee-chee-wee, a tormenting illness that caused the red blood cells to sickle into painful spikey thorns, causing agonizing torment as it ravaged her body. Before his father's mysterious and untimely disappearance, she rarely became ill, but lately a drafty room, a seemingly harmless cold, a slight change in weather, or slight fatigue and Noble would notice her rubbing her joints, wincing in pain. A heating pad covered her legs as she writhed in a fitful, restless sleep. It upset him to think of his mother's suffering. What's more, how could Noble comfort and aid a proud woman who would rather suffer quietly than admit she was sick or in pain?

When she finally did, it would be too late. She would have to go to the hospital, and he would see his mother with IVs and all kinds of tubes stuck in her frail and aching arms. And then he and Lark would have to stay with Aunt Byzantine and her cold, cruel cold stares and their mean cousins Tenebrous and Stone. And worst of all, his creepy Uncle Cypress. Sometimes his mother would be gone for days or even weeks. Once when the chee-wee-chee-wee was really bad, his mother Genesis was gone for nearly two months.

"Momma, are you hurting?" Noble asked, trying not to sound too concerned.

"No, my Little Man," she said. Her wise eyes took in his worry, and she gently touched his cheek. "It's your first day of school. You don't have to worry about me."

Just then, Lark swept into the kitchen modeling her new uniform, blue plaid skirt, baby blue blouse, and cadet blue sweater. Her mass of thick, wavy hair was parted down the middle into two Pochahontas-style braids that ended in curls. Leave it to Lark. She could make JC Penny nerd-ware seem like haut couture.

"Now you're sure you don't want me to give you two a ride to school?" his mother asked.

"No!" Lark and Noble yelled in unison.

"Uh, I mean that's okay, Momma" Noble said much more calmly. "We enjoy the bus ride to school." Being dropped off to school by your mother, a teacher, was tantamount to social suicide.

"Yeah, Momma," Lark joined in. "We wouldn't want to slow you down with your preparations and all on the first day." She flashed her Momma a winning smile. To most people, especially the boys in school or the ladies or elders at the church, this was all Lark needed to win their confidence. Genesis was immune to her daughter's charms, and this time, her radar zeroed in on Lark. Noble grinned wickedly as his mother waged a full frontal attack on his sister.

"Euphonia Lark Regalia Consonance Goodson!!" his mother yelled. Lark cringed at her mother's every crisply enunciated syllable of her Christian name.

"Momma, please don't call me that in front of everyone at school…" she whined.

"You better hope I don't pull a wash cloth and soap from my briefcase and scrub your face!" Genesis yelled. "Now go upstairs and clean the war paint from your face, Little Miss Paints-with-Brushes. And I don't want to hear about every other hoodlum-adolescent you call friend being allowed to wear cosmetics. Let me remind you that you are merely thirteen years old, not thirty!"

Lark stormed from the table and stomped upstairs to the bathroom.

Noble chuckled as he reached across the table to snatch two sausage links from Lark's plate. His mother glared at him.

"Whaaa??..." he mumbled over a mouthful of sausages and oatmeal. "She's not going to eat them. She's too busy trying to be Tyra Banks."

"Noble," she said more softly. "I want you to stay close to your sister today."

Noble was puzzled.

"Don't you mean she should stay close to me?" he asked, insulted. "I'm the oldest."

"Just humor me, Noble, and stay together." She said. "There's talk of abductions and kidnapping. One boy was reported missing last week, and this morning, Sister Rudolph informed me that Ruthie Mae's granddaughter may have been taken last night. Trust your instincts. If something feels dangerous, it is. Trust what you know to do is right."

Noble suddenly lost his appetite. *What is going on?* He wondered. But he couldn't help thinking that whatever it was had something to do with the feeling of dread he woke up with this morning. It became a more urgent lump in the bottom of his throat. He picked up the dishes from the table, scraped them into the garbage can, rinsed them, and placed them into the dish washer. Noble tried not to think of the mounting terror or his mother's cryptic warning.

Noble and Lark walked the half mile to the school bus stop on Highway 22 in silence. Lark poked out her pouty lips and started to kick at a pine comb in the road, but at the last minute changed her mind in fear of dirtying her polished shoes and thereby ruining her seemingly effortless look. The leaning live oaks formed a natural corridor along the winding, dusty road and groaned beneath the weight of all the Spanish moss that draped their limbs. Lark and Noble had walked along this road thousands of times, and Noble never tired of its beauty. Sometimes by looking up through the latticework of branches, he could spy rays of light filtering through the trees. Summers in Salvation, Georgia were beautiful. The pathway seemed enchanted when the sun's beams formed pools of light in the cool shadow of their shade. In winter the light took on richer, carroty and ochre hues, and he could not explain why that even on the coldest days the sight of its splendor would warm his heart. Other times, he got the impression that he was being watched when he passed by the majestic trees.

As usual, they stopped at a fork in the road that led to their neighbors' house, the Overbornes. His best friend Nicholas, or Nick as they called him, and his grandfather had lived there in the modest cottage for years. But since his mother's passing, the house was in utter disrepair. Shingles fell from the roof, the lawn was over grown, and a broken window was boarded up instead of replaced with a glass plane. Noble and Nick were in the same grade, barely. While Noble was a gifted honor student, Nick struggled to bring home C's and D's. His alcoholic grandfather yelled at him for being dumb, for the condition of the house, for being just like his no-good mother who had passed some years back, or not like her at all. And when he could find no reasons to berate Nick for, he would invent offenses and crimes. Because of his grandfather's drunken rages, Nick was timid, scrawny, and miserable. Nick hid these sad parts of his existence behind a biting sense of humor that got him into tons of trouble.

Nick made the street urchins in a Charles Dickens' novel look well nourished, wholesome, and happy. For if anyone got picked on and bullied in school, more than even Noble, it was Nick. But because of Nick's abrasive wit only those brave enough to risk social scrutiny under Nick's sharp tongue dared to insult him in person. Noble, Lark, and their mother loved him as if he were one of the family. And as far as they were concerned, he was.

"Nick!" called Noble. "C'mon. We're going to be late."

"Yeah, Nick!" cried Lark. "We can't miss the bus again. You know that bus driver gets a kick out of making you run."

Moments later, a wrinkled, lanky boy with ashen, chocolate skin trudged up the path. He could almost be called handsome with his high cheekbones and large, thick lashed dark eyes and lean muscles. Nick belted hand-me-down pants around his narrow frame. They were two sizes large and skimmed the top of his ankles. He hurried to button an oversized, shabby navy sweater around a worn and wrinkled white oxford shirt that was two sizes too small, revealing the ribs on his lean, muscular frame. In high school, mere physical beauty was not enough. The complete package for popularity included a smart, fashionable wardrobe along with key social standing. Nick had neither of these.

Noble pulled out a sandwich of the buttered toast and sausages saved from his breakfast from his back pack and handed them to Nick while Lark pulled a brush, a handkerchief, and a tube of hand lotion out of hers. Genesis packed Nick's breakfast and lunch everyday while they were in school and invited him over to dinner often. Nick loved their mother Genesis in ways that only one who missed his own mother could. He loved her cooking and drank in her attention, her mothering, and kind ways like a parched, withered plant to water. And she, sensing his need for affirmation and affection, loved him like one of her own. Genesis attended his parent-teacher conferences, cared for him when he fell ill, and would sneak him clothes if he could avoid his grandfather's notice. But unfortunately, when Mr. Overborne noticed Nick wearing anything new or decent, he would accuse him of stealing and beat him mercilessly after ripping, burning, or destroying the new item. For every moment of happiness, Genesis tried to give Nick, Nick's grandfather sought to snuff it out.

"Thanks Nobbs," Nick said as he stuffed half of the sandwich into his mouth.

"No problem, Man," Noble said as he tried not to get irritated at the way his sister fussed over his friend.

"Can you let the man come up for air, for goodness sake?!" he yelled.

Lark ignored him as she massaged some lotion on Nick's face, neck and hands, brushed his hair, and dusted off his sweater with her handkerchief. Both Lark and Noble stared at Nick's pants. Their eyes met briefly, and they both shook their heads. *Highwaters and oversized pants?* Noble thought. He finally surrendered to his sister to let her do her best, for he knew that Nick was in for complete and utter humiliation today. Suddenly his creased JC Penny navy pants and blue oxford shirt didn't scream NERD quite so loudly next to the pitiful picture Nick presented. He wasn't quite so angry that his mother insisted that they wear uniforms when everybody else wore their own fashions. And while Noble was neither happening nor cool, he realized he was not Nick. Noble felt a sudden pang of guilt at feeling better at Nick's misfortune. *After all, weren't they brothers?*

Nick basked in the attention that was Lark's makeover magic. Noble nudged Nick, reminding him not to drool over Lark as she, in an effort to improve Nick's appearance, tried to push up the arms of his sweater to no avail. Nick trailed Lark's every move with a vacant, listless look. Noble couldn't understand the crush Nick had on his sister --he tried not to vomit when he thought about it--, but he didn't hold it against his best friend. He just added the malady to the long list of Nick's injustices.

Once finished with Nick, Lark held her head higher, having forgotten the unfairness of not being allowed to wear whispering pink lip gloss and matching blush and hurried ahead to the bus stop to talk to her best friend Piccolo while Nick and Noble hung back and walked together. Noble snatched glances at Piccolo over Nick's shoulder as they talked. He could not help noticing that Piccolo had grown inches during the summer, making her taller, but the height did not take away from her willowy, womanish figure and slender curves. She tried inconspicuously to snatch glimpses of Noble as well, her golden eyes contrasted sharply with her caramel skin. Noble slung his backpack over his shoulder in nonchalance, pretending to be totally engrossed by its zipper and in Nick's conversation.

"Tell your momma thanks for the sausages," Nick said as he stuffed the remaining half in his mouth and spoke through mouthfuls.

"No need," Noble said as they caught up to Lark at the bus stop. "She knew maple flavored links are your favorite."

"You tryin' out for the team this year?" Nick asked.

"Don't know. " Noble said, pretending indifference. Instead he confided, "Yeah, I really want to, but I don't know if I'll make the cut."

"You have just as much a shot at it as anybody else," Nick said encouragingly.

Unlike Nick who was a natural athlete, Noble was horrible on the court. He was however, an excellent shooter. He part of Noble's brain that allowed him to shoot three pointers from across the court with ease froze in the heat of the game. He often forgot the rules of the sport. One of his most embarrassing moments was when in the last seconds of the neighborhood game he made a seemingly impossible shot in the opposing team's basket, losing the championship by three points before the ending buzzer. It was a moment that haunted Noble constantly, for the neighborhood fellows never let him forget it.

"We'll play a little one-on-one after school today," Nick offered. "That is if I can finish all my chores and Pops falls asleep early."

Noble knew that that meant that Mr. Overborne had an extra bottle of gin he bought with the money from Nick's paper route, and he would no doubt fall asleep earlier than his normal 7 p.m. drunken stupor.

Noble smiled at his friend as they boarded the bus, and as luck would have it, Ray Capers and his crew were not riding the bus this morning. They were on time, the bus driver was not in a foul mood, and Nick and Noble talked about Lebron James, Durant, and for once actually enjoyed the bus ride to school. *Maybe this year won't be so bad after all*, he thought. But of course, it was.

A Fight and a Summons on the First Day

Ray Capers waited patiently for Noble at the bus door as it pulled into the ramp of PS 119. Ray was hulking and enormous in a way that made Noble and other pubescent boys who had not quite grown into their lanky, adolescent frames feel vulnerable and afraid. In fact, to say that Ray Capers was enormous was like saying that the Titanic was a good-sized boat. He loomed over Noble menacingly, all six feet 4 inches and 280 lbs. of massive, bulging muscles and veins crammed unnaturally into a 15 year old frame.

Ray had blotchy, light brown skin, dark eyes, and two busy eyebrows that nearly formed a uni-brow. He looked that he was in dire need of a haircut, not to mention a shower, or an emergency visit to the dentist. As usual, Ray's gang, a dangerous assortment of angry, failing and rebellious teens with tattoos and gold teeth who were two cut classes and one suspension away from dropping out, accompanied Ray on his bullying exploits.

"Well, if it isn't our resident punk snitch," Ray said peering up at Noble at the top of the exit ramp stairs. As if on cue, the gang snickered and laughed. Some of the throng leaned against the wall, arms crossed, viewing Ray's bullying, the first of many. Noble commanded his feet to walk inch by inch off the bus. Besides, staying on the bus was futile: there were students anxious to see the first bit of excitement of the school year, and they pressed in behind him, urging him to his doom on the bus ramp.

Noble grimaced at Ray's words. *Snitch.* When he and Ray were in third grade together, a heavier and meaner fourth grader, with red hair and freckles, kicked Ray in the stomach and punched him over and over and over again in the hallway one afternoon. The red headed bully had called Ray a nigger, and Ray who didn't respond to many words, incensed, reacted violently. Noble saw a floating demon, colorless except for its red eyes, hover over Ray and the red headed bully, its eyes gleaming wildly in maniacal glee. Another demon, its leering, black twin, presided over the fighting. It was strange to Noble that a two syllable slur could cause the display of viciousness and ferocity.

If Noble had not run to get the coach, Ray would have undoubtedly lost more of the much needed IQ points that had gotten him through middle school. The memory was chilling to Noble for many reasons. In addition to the ferocious display, Noble had seen two malignant spirits that day, hovering over the two fighting boys. Black mists and shadow gathered in the corners of Noble's eyes. The spirits' eyes glowed red with yellow slits, and when they noticed Noble watching them, they winked and jeered.

"We are Prejudice and Fury," they spoke in ragged whispers. "When there is ignorance, we strike! When there is anger, we strike! Only few can see us. We see *you*, Son of Light."

Noble shivered. The gym had gotten very cold, and the more the boys fought, the colder the room became. The hovering spirits also seemed to have an effect on the watching crowd. The students grew restless and angry. And violent. At only eight years old, Noble did the only thing he knew to do to not only break up the onslaught by the bully, but also to prevent a potential free-for-all and public melee. But instead of earning Ray's appreciation, Noble earned his constant ridicule and torment throughout elementary and middle school. High school seemed no different.

"Did you miss me?" Ray asked. Again, Ray's crew snickered.

"No," Noble said, noticing the gang moved into positions that seemed to block all avenues of possible escape. "Can't say that I have. Though I can't believe you were all that lonely with your... boys." Noble nodded to Ray's menacing entourage. "You're the only bully I know who travels with a crew of juvenile-delinquent, hype men." Noble hoped his voice projected confidence when he was really trying to quell the desire to vomit and a pounding heartbeat in his throat.

"That ain't what I heard," Ray said. His nostrils flared and he pressed his colossal frame against Noble's face. "I heard you been running scared and dying to make up and be friends." Again, the gang of miscreants guffawed and jeered.

"Is that what you heard, *Tangarey*?" Noble said. Instantly, he regretted taunting Ray by saying his real name as he heard the snickering and giggling from the students who pressed behind him on the bus ramp and those who had yet to exit the bus. It was a well-known "secret joke" amongst the students in the school that Marva Capers, a well-known drunk, had given her children of different fathers the names of her favorite drinks, Margarita, Kovassier, and Tangaray Gin. No one would dare to laugh at his ridiculous name in front of Ray Caper's face.

"I mean Ray," Noble said realizing that as much as he wanted to, he could not take back calling Ray his real name, and that Ray who had had the jeering approval of his miscreant gang, would have to beat up Noble to save face in front of them.

"You want to call out names, Bitch?" Ray asked, the last two words ending in a growl. He pressed his muscular frame even closer to Noble and pushed Noble roughly against the bus, grabbing him by the throat.

Noble's feet just cleared the stairs. Noble pushed Ray back gaining his footing, stood up, and squared his shoulders. If he was going to get beaten down, he was going to take it like a man. He clinched his fists, remembering the one-two combination his father had taught him before he left for the Middle East months ago. Then, it had been fun boxing with his father in the backyard.

"Keep your eyes open," his father taunted as he playfully jabbed Noble.

Looking at Ray who looked less the juvenile delinquent and more like a wall of fury, Noble wondered if he would be able to get in at least one good punch before Ray pummeled him. Noble managed to connect his fist with Ray's jaw. Ray did not flinch. He smiled, rubbing his jaw and punched Noble in the stomach. Noble doubled over, losing all of the air in his stomach and chest.

A part of his consciousness seemed to drift out of him and float over him as Ray and his cronies punched, kicked, and slammed his stomach, back, and ribs. The dream-Noble hovered closer in curiosity. *So this is what it feels and looks like to get beaten up. Well, there is a first for everything.* The dream-Noble hovered free as the physical Noble went farther and farther down a dark tunnel of pain. Noble was on the ramp now, drawn up in a fetal position. Most of the gang, bored of the ten to one assault and wary of one more suspension that would lead to certain expulsion, fell back and watched what Ray would do next.

But then Noble, both the dream-Noble and the physical one, melded back together. At the bottom of the tunnel of pain and fury, Noble sensed a disquieting change in the fabric of reality. It was not unlike the shimmering of heat waves in the dead of summer or the rustling surface of rapid, boiling water, except that there was a distinctive, unnatural chill peculiar for mid-August. The air above Ray first rippled, then bulged and puckered, and parted to reveal a monstrous-sized, rotting, green fist, of which bore ragged, yellowed nails and coarse, hairy knuckles. The tightly clutched fist opened to release its treasure: a hellish cache of gigantic cockroaches with sharp stingers and pincers in the same sickly, gangrenous color.

The cockroaches swarmed in the air, their pincers poised for biting and stinging, a frightening and unnatural cloud eclipsing the summer sun. They swarmed for Ray's forehead. Each ghastly insect fell on their prey with sickening accuracy. Only Noble seemed to notice each horrific thud and plop as the cockroaches seized upon Ray's brow, head, and shoulders and stung. Ray, who did not seem to notice the monstrous hand, the unnatural eclipse, or even the freaky cockroaches, sank to his knees and vomited on the parking lot. He writhed and gasped in agony, grabbing his brow, swollen with welts. Some of the cockroaches burrowed beneath Ray's flesh, and Noble saw traveling lumps that moved all over his body. Ray quivered in agonizing silence.

Beneath the bulging muscles, beneath the shrunken stance of terror, Noble saw. A glimmer of memory flitted through. A smaller Ray and his sister Rita, ages four and two, appeared. The child Ray cringed in terror. His mother's snoring form lay sprawled over the couch and onto the floor, her legs splayed in unladylike angles beneath a booze-stained, neon pink, polyester mini-skirt. Alize and mustard vied for first place in a stain race across her open mini-skirt. Ray and Rita, torn between their urgent hunger, they had not eaten in days, and the fear of waking their sleeping mother, spent the early morning hours quietly searching for food.

An hour's search yielded a half-empty box of stale Toasted Oat Smacks and a wrinkled bag of potato chips that were two years beyond their expiration date. The young Ray did not have to read the expiration date, at age four he couldn't, to know that the contents inside the old, wrinkled bag were spoiled. They young Ray was used to living half-starved and unkempt and always disappointed. He learned early to be outraged at the pitying glances of concerned adults but never directed his anger at the source of his young misery: his partying, alcoholic mother. He bore her disappointing performance as a guardian with a devotion and fervor almost as strong as the love for his sister, who he had already begun caring for with an intensity well beyond his four years. Ray, Tangeray, named by his mother in a drinking binge, had already begun to stoop under the oppressive weight of his cares.

A large, hissing, albino cockroach, six inches long, had already lay claim to the spoil of stale Toasted Oats Smacks. Once Ray had opened the box and found the cockroach hissing and indignant, he shrank away in fear.

Noble saw Ray, the hulking teen who threatened to hurt him in ways Noble would never forget, with a new clarity and understanding that breached sympathy. He realized that Ray didn't need his contempt, pity, or fear. Ray needed his compassion. Noble offered it now.

The memory, a Technicolor image superimposed on the backdrop of roiling, rustling air, flickered once, twice, and then vanished. Stiff with pain and bruises, Noble pulled himself to his feet, thinking to lash out at the monstrous cockroaches. He just wanted to rid himself of the danger. He considered the terrorized boy in the memory and spoke.

"Ray," Noble said. Ray whimpered and trembled, staring at the anguishing memory that Noble knew only Ray and he could see. "I know you're scared of cockroaches. Since you were a baby. Frankly, I don't like them either...." Ray did not respond. Noble grunted and tasted the blood on his split lip. He grabbed his sore stomach, trying to ignore the explosion of pain in his belly and ribs. Seeing Ray's cowering form, he tried again.

"I'm afraid of them, too," Noble said. "I'm not trying to hurt you, Man. I'm just going to get them off of you. Okay? Can you let me do that for you? Ray?" Somewhere in the hulking, simpering, cowering mass, Ray nodded. Noble searched for a spot on Ray's skin that was as free of the hellish creatures as possible. An inspiration born of a higher wisdom seized Noble. He suddenly knew three things:

1. The attack on Ray was as much an attack on his psyche and emotions as it was physical.

2. That only he and Raw were aware of what was happening. Noble glanced at Ray's gang, the students on the ramp, and the cheering throng on the bus. Time, apparently frozen, had made still-like pictures of the screaming, cheering students whose faces stared blankly into space.

3. That Noble possessed some supernatural powers and that somehow it was up to him to use them to save Ray and himself.

He acted now. As he searched Ray's trembling figure, he found it, a bare area of skin free of the insects, the brow just over the right eye and a patch of exposed cheek. He stretched out his hands, and as soon as he did, noticed a ray of heat radiating from them. It didn't burn him, but Noble hoped that he could burn the hellish creatures. As soon as he thought it, a stream of searing, red heat spewed from his hands. Noble directed the stream over to the roaches. To his surprise, the hellish creatures ran from it. Encouraged by the bugs' retreat, Noble ran his hands over Ray's head and shoulders. The insects shrieked in agony as they burned and crackled in fire. The lumps under Ray's skin flattened and then vanished. The space on Ray's face left by the retreating, monstrous bugs widened. Seeing his opportunity, Noble continued. He struck Ray squarely on the right cheek. The bugs flew from their fiery perch away from Ray, and those who were not able to escape, hissed and squealed, burning into ash.

"Leave him alone," Noble yelled. And to his utter amazement, a beam, a ray of warm light emitted from his outstretched palm onto the red whelp left by the slap on Ray's face, prompting the cockroaches to halt their terrorizing attack on Ray and fly from their perch on his head ... towards him.

"Oh No!" Noble yelled, shaking his head. For a moment, Noble lost his nerve as the bugs lunged for him. Liquid fire burned his neck and left cheek. Noble slapped the bugs away from him and raised his hand again. He stood his ground and the beam of light formed a shield around him and Ray. The bugs halted inches from his feet on the ground and the shield around him and Ray. They began to hiss and click and buzz. Noble fought a compulsion to scratch incessantly. Never had he seen such large numbers of bugs, especially the nightmarish creatures that hovered around him. They did not harm Noble, but formed freakish and elegant lines and loops on the bus ramp pavement all while buzzing and clicking. In seconds, the clicking and hissing stopped and the fiendish cockroaches burst into flames leaving a peculiar black powder on the ground that spelled out a cryptic message:

Noble Goodson, Son of Light,
You are hereby summoned to appear
before the Council of Elders
on the 31nd day of August in the year of 2009
To determine your eligibility for service to the
Light

The same icy wind blew the ashes into a small funnel, not unlike a dirt devil. The funnel flew back into the outstretched monstrous hand. Once more it formed a tightly clutched fist which retreated into the wrinkle that disturbed the fabric of what used to be the normal world. And then it was gone. Once more the students were buzzing with excitement and chatter.

"Dang, Noble," another girl from the crowd said, Myrna Staples. "I didn't know you had it in you!"

"Yeah Noble," said another. "We were sure we'd have to call paramedics. I thought it was a sure bet. I lost ten dollars! How did you do it?"

Noble looked around at the cheering students, the whimpering Ray Capers, and the sudden change in the weather as if none of the crazy things had ever happened. The monstrous hand, the weather, the hellish cockroaches, they all vanished. And even Noble began to wonder if he had all but imagined them.

Melody Stevens, his secret crush since third grade, her jet black hair braided into corn rows that ended in curls down her back, eyed him with a new look of admiration, and not the amused side-ways stare she ordinarily met him with. None of them seemed to notice what had just happened.

Another spectator from the crowd slapped Noble on the back.

"When he wakes up, I feel sorry for you," he said.

Creep Jeffrey Capers? That was the least of his worries, Noble thought.

Lark and Nick, who had been in the rear of the bus and separated by the throng of students when Noble and Ray were attacked, rushed to Noble's side.

"Are you okay, Nobby?" Lark asked. Her face was pale and she had the same fear in her eyes that he knew his must have shown.

"Are you okay, Man?" Nick asked.

"Did you see th-that?" Noble asked.

"Not now, Noble," Nick said. "There may be more of them around."

"More of who – or WHAT?!" Noble screeched.

Both Lark and Nicholas grabbed Noble by the arms and half-supported, half-dragged him into the third wing hallway, an unpopular part of school, partly because of its location to the pissy boys' bathroom and partly because it was away from the main activity of the school.

Noble couldn't stop scratching now. His anxiety attack was in full swing.

"WHAT WAS THAT?" he yelled.

Both Nick and Lark looked desperately at each other before returning hesitant stares.

"WHAT WAS THAT?" he repeated.

Lark stared at Nick before answering.

"Why do you look at each other?" Noble asked. "As if you know something I don't? I asked you both a question!"

"You've been summoned," Lark mumbled. Then she cleared her throat and repeated, "You've been summoned."

Noble gave them both a hysterical look and then collapsed.

Noble awakened to the faint ticking of an old, mahogany, grandfather clock. He lay on a worn, but comfortable, brown, leather couch. How long he had been here or even how he even ended up in the counselor's office, he did not know.

Noble rose slowly, gingerly rubbing the lump on the back of his head. He grabbed the tender areas in his back and stomach. He remembered the ten on one fight with Ray and his gang, but he didn't remember hitting his head. In fact, the last thing he did remember was Lark and Nick's worried faces as they leaned over him, trying to calm him down. They mentioned something about a "summons".

Noble was surprised to see a fire crackling merrily in a fireplace in mid-August. Oddly, the room had a supernatural coolness, and he found the fire's warmth comforting. Its warm glow provided enough light in the dark office so that he could make out shelves and shelves of books that lined the walls of this small, yet cozy room. Noble surveyed his surroundings. He sat upright slowly, wincing as the back of his head throbbed a freestyle percussion solo.

"This must be the counselor's office," Noble said.

Somehow, he imagined the room of Mrs. Papagallo to be plastered with corny posters like "You Control Your Own Destiny" or "Your Future Matters". But instead he found that the walls that weren't crammed with books bore hundreds and hundreds of postcards: Welcome to Peru! Greetings from Madagascar and Wish You Were Here in Fiji!

An ancient secretary made of the same glowing mahogany as the grandfather clock took up most of the rest of the office. The door opened. Noble tried to appear as normal as possible, stilling himself for the questions he knew must come. He frantically searched his mind for logical explanations to account for the erratic behavior of what must have seemed like a total nervous breakdown in the school parking lot.

Pure instinct warned him that if he confided to Mrs. Papagallo the spectacle he witnessed today, she would not hesitate to refer him to the nearest psychiatric hospital or at least send a county social worker out to the house. To his astonishment, however, the person who entered the room carrying a tray of assorted cookies and mugs of steaming hot chocolate was not the short and stout Mrs. Papagallo but the limping school janitor, Abe Cedarian.

Mr. Cedarian looked like a living replica of Frederick Douglass, or at least a close cousin. The elderly man carefully set the tray down on the secretary before limping over to Noble. His glowing, bronzed face, not unlike polished copper, bent down to examine Noble. Noble who had never been this close to the janitor and had definitely never been in his office -*Did janitors even have offices?* -did not find himself afraid. And although his hair was a wiry halo of frayed, wispy cotton, his smooth, unwrinkled skin and twinkling, dark brown eyes belied a youthfulness that Noble noticed in most mischievous children.

"How are you, young Goodson?" Mr. Cedarian asked.

"Okay, I guess," Noble answered with apprehension.

"You've suffered a nasty fall," Mr. Cedarian said pointing to the area that was the painful, throbbing goose egg on Noble's head. "May I have a look at that please?" he asked.

Grateful that Mr. Cedarian did not question him about the freaky incident or his passing out, Noble leaned his head forward.

Mr. Cedarian gently touched the back of Noble's head. To Noble's surprise, he felt a curious, warming sensation where Mr. Cedarian's calloused fingers touched him. The pain, his carefully hidden hysteria, the bumps and bruises and hurt places, and uncertainty suddenly melted away. Noble touched his head.

"Hey, the knot… It's gone!" he said in amazement.

He gasped and looked at Mr. Cedarian. Mr. Cedarian returned his stare. Almost at once, Noble felt at peace and energized, like he had just woken up from a refreshing nap, without the recurring nightmare.

"What?" Noble asked.

"Noble Adjani Goodson, Son of Light," he answered. "It is a pleasure to finally meet you. I have so much to explain."

3

Abe Cedarian
and the Trial

Noble stared intently at Abe and waited. At last he would have
some answers. At last, he would find out what the recurring
nightmares prophesied, of what his mother's cryptic comments
meant. At last, someone would explain all the unexplainable things he
saw today, and the undefined, creepy things that lurked in the periphery
of his vision.

"We don't have much time, Noble. So listen closely," Abe said. "You
are about to enter the first in a series of tasks that begin your initiation
into the Society of Light. Your father's disappearance, the disturbing
things you see and sense around you, what happened with Ray Capers today, these are not mere coincidences, but portents, signs of your destiny
of what is to come. Noble Goodson, you are descended from a long line
of Light Workers, your mother and father before you, and their ancestors
before them. You are an instrument of the timeless battle between Light
and Dark, of Good and Evil. It is yet unclear as to what your role in this

battle will be, but it is a very significant one. For through your efforts, your actions as a vessel of power for the Light, prisoners will be set free, the hungry fed, the wearied comforted, the confused made sensible, and the lost recovered, the cursed set free...."

"You've been given very special powers as an instrument of the Light and now the Light which has sheltered and blessed you, seeks you to fulfill the purpose for which you have been formed. Salvation needs a champion. The Darkness will continue to snatch innocents until someone with a pure heart, someone who believes, can find the Nazarene Tear and stop the Darkness before it is too late. And because the Light calls you, the Darkness hounds you, becoming forever your powerful and relentless enemy. Hence, you were summoned by the Dark today. It recognized your potential as a Light Worker. Such is the lot of all who endeavor to answer the Call. Today, young Noble, you face your Trial...."

"My trial?" Noble asked. "What have I done wrong?"

"That is the very question that lies before you today. Look deep, Noble. There are many possibilities in the word. Things are not always what they seem. And yet, you always have the power of choice. Choose wisely. Many have failed before you, chosen amiss. Others have failed no matter how honorable their intentions. If my suspicions are correct, I believe there is enough of the Light within you to help you make the right choices in your trial and in the battle to come."

Trial, choices, Light Workers, battles.... it was all too much, Noble thought. Yet Noble knew he had to choose carefully.

"Where are we going?" Noble asked.

"Not where," Abe answered. "For where we are going has no boundaries that can limit it as an actual place and no time to limit it as a when. It is between dimensions, realms, even though these very words are limiting in their naming. It is a meeting place between good and evil. What you are about to hear and witness very few have ever seen, and fewer still ever will. Take my hand."

Noble once again obeyed Abe, offering his trembling hand to the

Wise One. Abe's grip was surprisingly strong for his age. The moment Abe's rough, weathered hands seized his, he felt a rush of warmth followed by a surge of power. He felt comforted, reassured. Noble's trembling hand steadied itself in Abe's strong grasp.

"Clear your mind," Abe instructed. "Sometimes it helps to close your eyes. Fewer distractions."

Noble closed his eyes.

"Now call out with your voice and with your mind," Abe said.

"Call?" Noble asked. "What am I supposed to say?"

"Focus on the word, Noble." Abe said. His clutch tightened around Noble's throbbing fingers. Noble frantically searched his mind for a word to guide him to a place that could not be described as a where, or a time that could not be limited by a when. He took a deep breath. This was weird. Too weird.

"Summons," Noble mumbled. The words were hollow and flat. He heard a faint echo. It chided him of his silliness. Noble stole a sideways, sheepish glance toward Abe. Nervous giggles escaped his lips.

Abe shook his head and in spite of the circumstances, merriment sparkled in his gentle brown eyes.

"I'm afraid you'll have to do better than that, Noble," Abe said. "Answer with your mind as well as your voice. Yell if you have to."

"I, Noble Goodson, come to answer the summons!" he yelled. He closed his eyes tighter and dared himself to believe and not giggle or suck his teeth, even though every ounce of his being wanted to laugh at the idea of how silly he sounded. How crazy he must have looked: A wacky teen and a janitor yelling at the wall. Nonsense! He waited in silence.

And then he heard it. First, the sound of a mighty and horrible rushing wind, not unlike the deadly onslaught of an attacking hurricane he had heard on the Weather Channel before. But worse. It was a shrill whistling, piercing the howl and the roar. The frightful din came closer, encircling him, snatching him up in its mischievous currents. The torrents, like cold biting leather, stung at his face and arms.

Noble opened his eyes to an overwhelming blackness. The mahogany clock, the post cards, the desk, the very floor he stood upon were all gone. And he was twirling and spinning, spinning and twirling, like a helpless plaything of the angry wind tossed about mercilessly. There was no here or where. There was no when. Just blackness and the horrible, rushing wind.

Abram grasped Noble. In his mind he heard the Wise One's rich voice, and he held on tighter to his hand. Like a drowning victim, Noble snatched out to it in return, hoping to escape being overtaken by the storm.

"This is where I leave you, Noble" Abram spoke softly, comfortingly.

"Leave?" Noble called out to Abram with his mind. Trying to suppress the rising panic in his throat and stomach, he listened.

"One of the defenses against the Darkness is secrecy. By revealing my association to you, I render myself ineffective, incapable of helping you against the Dark. So you must tell no one of our meetings, especially not your mother. Only disclose information to those of whom you are certain. The Darkness uses ties, relationships and affections against you. Your mother has suffered, is suffering enough."

Noble paused and considered the old man's words. The monstrous wind made his shirt snap and crack in its currents. He knew that he could not mistake his words. Noble suppressed a shudder, swallowed hard in desperation, and nodded.

"Are you ready?" Abe asked.

Noble nodded again. And then, making up his mind to confront whatever lay ahead, he added. "Yes." In his mind, he tried to send Abram a mental picture of a field of sunflowers, reaching, stretching toward a benevolent sun. The sun was made of warm, glowing ochre, crimson, and the most unique shade of peach he'd ever seen. Words could not describe the beauty of its vision. Somehow Noble felt in his heart that sunflowers were dear to his kind teacher. Again, somehow he also knew that Abe had mentored many Light Workers before him. Knowing this, he gave each sunflower the face of a child, the children Abe had taught before him. Each sunflower stretched toward the sun's bathing warmth. Noble felt Abram take in a sharp breath and then smile. If he didn't know any better, he thought Abram was crying.

"You are mighty indeed, Son of Light," Abram said. "You will forever be blessed because of your kindness, like your mother and father before you. It is true. You are the One, and I am honored to have known you."

Noble was confused at Abram's words. They sounded so final, and yet he knew deep within his soul that he would see wise and gentle Abe Cedarian again.

"We are at war, Noble," Abe said. "Make no mistake."

And then the horrible wind, the blackness, the biting, and Abe were gone. Noble's body crashed upon the cold surface of a granite floor. He struggled to his feet, nursing a sore rib. In the glaring spotlight of an otherwise dark room, Noble gazed about him. His face smarted from the wind's painful welts. He noticed that what he stood on was a dais, a floating dais. Slowly, carefully, he crept to its edge. His brand new white Nikes, given to him by his mother as part of his back to school wardrobe, now ragged and torn and missing a shoelace, dislodged crumbling black pebbles from its periphery. Noble noticed that the pebbles fell down, down, down into more blackness. He strained to hear where they would finally hit ground. He didn't.

"Noble Goodson!" a voice called. Noble struggled to shield his eyes from the blinding light, trying to locate who or what the voice came from.

"Yes," Noble answered.

"Noble Goodson, son of the servants of Light. You have come to answer the summons. How do you plead?

"Plea?" Noble asked.

The darkness thinned out, shifting to resettle into pools of dim, obscure light and murky shadow. Noble could make out that he was not alone. There were hooded figures all around him, assembled in what looked like an oval court room. The pools of light softly outlined figures in gleaming white robes. Pools of shadow hid besmirched and benighted, robed figures. Noble sensed evil in the shadows, barely contained. But unlike a courtroom there were no opposing sides. The good and evil sat together, and the voice that called out to him seemed to emanate from all around him instead as from one person.

At once a transparent image, like a hologram played out the nightmarish scene of the incident with Ray Capers today. Noble watched as his hand slapped Ray and his body crumpled to the asphalt. There were indistinct murmurs and hisses coming from the hooded figures.

"Guilty!" one screamed. He noticed that the hooded speaking figure pointed at him. His hand, scaly, and hideous, was more of a claw.

"How do you plea?" the voice boomed.

Noble turned around as other hissing figures cried guilty.

"Guilty!" cried another hissing figure.

"Punish him!" accused another.

"It's not what it looks like. That's not how it really went down!" Noble cried.

At his words, the dais plunged ten feet. Noble careened dangerously towards the edge. He tried to remember Abram's advice of choosing wisely.

"Who speaks for the accused?" the voice asked.

A raven, gleaming and magnificent flew from the throng. It lighted on the dais next to Noble. The moment it lighted, its body transformed. The wings folded behind him and melted into nothingness. The bird elongated, glimmered, and grew. It became a hooded figure of a man cloaked in an ancient, brown robe.

"I do," the man said.

"Who speaks?" The voice boomed. "Reveal yourself."

"I, Blaze Barrister, speak for the boy. He has the gift of compassion and the gift of sight." The man threw back his hood to reveal a thin and emaciated figure not unlike his father. He shared the same copper skin and the same hazel eyes as his father.

Could it be? Noble thought.

No sooner did he think the words did he notice that the mysterious, cloaked figure, certainly just under seven feet, towered over his father's six foot six inches. His shoulders were not as wide nor as strong as his father's but strong none the less. And when Noble whispered his Uncle's name, Napthalim, the stranger lightly brushed his finger across his lips.

"Noble is friend to animals, kind to the poor, compassionate to the hurting. These are why he should be a son of Light," Blaze the stranger continued.

"On the other hand," a hissing whisper uninterrupted, "Noble Goodson is clumsy, rash, and acts out before thinking. He has no heart—he barely has a brain. Listen to the testimony of one who is closest to him."

The air shimmered and roiled. It reminded him of the rustling of boiling water, as if every molecule in the air around him wavered and shook. Even with the shimmering, he could make out his mother's face.

"He is not ready!" she yelled. "He is no match for the darkness. He is merely a boy, a boy compelled to walk in his father's footsteps. And now that Aro is gone, who will guide him? Who will mentor him? Who will protect him? It grieves my heart to say this, but Noble is not ready."

Noble's throat felt dry. For a moment, words deserted him. Never had his mother spoken with so little confidence in him. It hurt him. It stung him in ways he could not put into words. And because his mother had lost faith in him, he spoke loudly and angrily.

"I Noble Goodson accept the trial, the assignment, and the quest set before me, and if I should die trying, so be it."

Many hooded figures groaned in approval. Others hissed and screeched. Noble felt he had made the right decision. The missing children needed him, his father needed him, and so did his mother. A nagging sensation goaded him to fight the Darkness, whoever or whatever it was. He was right to be afraid, but what else could he do? After all, the

Trial, as Abe Cedarian had warned him, was nothing but a quest or a summons to answer. Noble felt compelled to answer it. The Trial was no longer a mystery, and Noble felt amazingly calm and settled in his decision. Noble wondered what would have happened to him if he had reacted to the accusations and chosen to defend himself. Would he have plummeted to his death? Is that what Abe meant by the others "choosing amiss"? Did the others fail to see the positive aspects of the word?

No matter what, he would rescue the Innocent, he would find the Nazarene Tear, and he would heal his mother, no matter how little confidence she felt in him. He would prove her wrong.

"Very well," the voice that sounded like dry leaves and a snake's hissing in the wind. "The choice is yours, and once you have chosen there is no going back, even to the point of death."

"Very well, Son of Darkness," Noble said. The monstrous hissing growled and groaned more. Noble had no idea how he knew what to call the hissing stranger, but his heart told him it was important that he did.

Blaze Barrister smiled, but not before he sought out Noble's eyes with his own, wishing him courage and strength. His gaunt chest swelled with pride as he considered his brave nephew.

In the shimmering image, Genesis threw her hands into her face and wept mournful, woeful tears. Her shoulders shook with each racking sob. A mysteriously cloaked figure wrapped his hands around her to console her. Noble instantly hated this mysterious man, this stranger who felt familiar enough to wrap his mother in his arms. There was more to him than he was willing to admit, and he had the distinct impression that she was in danger. The shimmering gradually faded away leaving nothing but the sound of her wailing. Soon even the wailing dissipated.

Suddenly the dais, the dimly lit hall, the hooded figures, even his uncle disappeared, and he felt as if he was drugged and falling into a deep sleep. When he awakened, he found himself back in the janitor's office in Abe's comfortable couch. Weird that a janitor's office would have all the creature comforts of a cozy office, but Noble didn't complain.

Abe's cotton hair and gleaming, bright eyes with nearly no iris to separate the cedar brown shone with pride as he sat with his legs crossed gracefully in a high back chair in front of the crackling fire. His wrinkle-free, smooth skin and twinkling eyes made him seem more like an adolescent than an ancient one, a Wise One.

"Well done, Young Goodson," Abe exclaimed. "While I am glad to see that you made it back in one piece, this in no way means victory. We are on the eve of a long, arduous battle. It is begun.

"Take this," Abe said.

He placed a rough, burlap sack in his hand. Noble pulled the string that opened its contents. Inside he noticed a handful of glowing seeds.

"Lesson one," Abe said. "These are called mustard seeds. This begins your first lesson in faith. Light workers use these in dire circumstances to fight the Darkness. Whenever you need a miracle, whenever you need to escape, hold one of these up, ask for what you need, and believe. There's also a touch stone ---"

Noble's eyes were heavy. He fought to stay awake in spite of the fight, his feinting, and his Trial. He knew that what Abe explained was important, but he was just too tired.

"I think that's enough for today, Noble," Abe said. His eyes twinkled in the firelight. "I'm going to *speak* you home. In our world, that is the world of Luminaries and Lightworkers, we speak things into being and they occur. This will take some practice for you, but you will soon learn. While you were in the Meeting Place, time passed in the real world. Sometimes when you visit the other realms, time will pass and sometimes, it will stay still. I allowed time to pass for you because I figured you would not be up for a full day of school once you've survived and accepted your trial. When you find yourself in your own bed without having walked home, you will know that my words hold truth. But before I send you, hear me."

"Here's your excuse for missing school; it's been glamoured, affected so that whoever gazes upon it will not only excuse your absence, but will willingly give you all that you need to continue in your classes. You will need to meet me here at 6 am Saturday mornings to begin your training. The Darkness does not rest. You will need to train your spiritual senses as well as your physical ones. The Darkness takes no enemies, not one. Remember that. And above all, do not ever let your mother know what we do. She knows that you have accepted your trial now. She will be worried. She is needed in this spiritual community of ours. Healing and Discernment are but a few of the many gifts the Light has endowed her as a Handmaiden of the Light. Your being hurt would distract her from her duties. Your death would only kill her. Mark my words, Noble. This is very important. Let no one know you know me. Let no one know you train with me. Let no one know I am a Light Worker, except for those that I reveal to you are in the Light, such as your sister and Nicholas. Our very lives depend on it. Do you understand, Son of Light? Too many lives are at stake. And now I will send you home."

Abe held out his hand toward Noble on the couch and spoke loudly.

"I command all that is Light and Good to take the young Light Warrior home. Guard him from harm and keep him safe from the Darkness and from the allies of the Usurper. Keep young Lark and Nicholas safe. Comfort his mother in the battle that is to come. To Home."

As the Wise One spoke, the office seemed to melt around him until all that was left were his words. They echoed in the walls of his room as they became more solid. At last, even those faded. Noble marveled at how the real world seemed to have abandoned him today. He looked down at his body fully clothed in his favorite plaid pajamas and felt the soft, cool firmness of the mattress underneath him. He was back in his room, in his own bed, when only moments before he had stood in Abe's office. It was like a bad joke, a freakish nightmare, but Noble distinctly remembered Abe giving him the burlap bag containing the mustard seeds and the touch stone, an omen against evil. He held the glowing amber stone in a tight grip in his hand, wondering what it would do before drifting off to sleep.

4

A Night Out Turns Horribly Wrong

As usual, the parking lot behind Rich's Department store teemed with adolescents. Salvation boasted several teen social clubs, an arcade, and an adolescent night club that closed at 9:00 pm week nights and 11:00 pm Friday and Saturday nights. There was also the mall that stayed open until 10:00 pm, three movie theaters, and a skating rink on Highway 70. But as many youth who believe the activities that adults set up for them are boring, the teens of Salvation found the Rich's parking lot a popular "hangout" on Wednesday night.

Rap music blared from the open doors and windows of many parked cars. The booming drumbeat and deafening bass intensified the cursing and anger of rap artists and rattled the tinted windows. Adolescent boys and girls nodded and bobbed their heads to the seductive, pulsating rhythm. Some couples gyrated shamelessly, intoxicated by cheap liquor and angry, explicit lyrics. Bands of girls undulated their serpentine waists in suggestive invitations. Some boys answered the invitation of their undulating hips and led them into the seclusion of cars, dark trucks, or dark corners and alleys. Other intimate, smaller groups talked quietly amongst themselves as they leaned against their cars, dragged on cigarettes, and drank their beer. Others nodded their heads to the cynicism and hopelessness spewed by angry rap artists. Lust, a scantily clad demon in a black, leather corset and mini-skirt gyrated among them, her pale green skin glistening with the effort of her wild maneuvers, her forked tongue wavering between her parted, blood red lips. Her brother Drunkenness, clothed in a black leather duster and leather pants, raised a jeweled encrusted cup to her in mock salute from his leaning stance on a parked car. He waved his green hand with polished red talons at a group of teens leaning against the tinted windows of a parked truck. Crates of beer and bottled gin materialized. The teens already intoxicated due to two and a half hours of booze binging, drunkenly cheered at their mysterious good fortune. Drunkenness joined his sister Lust in a lascivious, dancing threesome with an intoxicated fifteen year old he had drugged with the essence of poppies moments before. He shared a wicked smile with his sister.

While her parents slept, Piccolo sneaked out of her bedroom window to join Paige and Lauren outside.

"Are you sure I'll be home before 11:00?" Piccolo asked.

"Are you sure I'll be home before 11:00?" Lauren repeated, raising her voice an octave higher to mimic Piccolo's high pitched tone. Piccolo winced at Lauren's mocking tone.

"It's just that I have to… I need to be home before my parents wake up," Piccolo said. Piccolo had never snuck out of her room or disobeyed her parents, but ever since she spent less time with Lark and her new, best friend Page started hanging around the school bad-girl Lauren, Piccolo found herself becoming the type of daughter her parents did not want her to be.

"We'll get the baby back home before her mommy and daddy wake up." Lauren said. Piccolo groaned inwardly and kept silent while she suffered her friends to apply eyeliner and lipstick to her face. She had never worn makeup before either but thought better against saying so to avoid being called a baby for that, too.

Thirty minutes later Piccolo stood alone in the Rich's parking lot while Paige shared a drink with two boys. Piccolo watched as her new best friend gulped back the contents of a red plastic cup and giggled. If only Lark wasn't so busy. Lately, she saw less and less of her Lark, her best friend since Pre-K, and she never seemed to have time for her. She remembered that just before school started, they had spent countless weekend slumber bashes at the Goodson home: buttered popcorn, mani-pedis, girl talk, and Dance Party on the Wii. Piccolo remembered with unshed tears that they had so much fun dancing the night away in their pajamas and talking about boys. Now, Piccolo didn't know what she had done to offend her only real friend. When she called Lark, her messages always went to voicemail.

One of the two boys, a pimply teen with gold teeth and shades, draped his arm about her shoulders while pouring more of a clear, brown colored liquid from an unmarked bottle. Lauren had disappeared the moment they had arrived, slinking off with an older teen, maybe in his twenties, with a perfect, movie-star smile and dimples. The tattoo of a demon branded the biceps of flawless, sepia skin. The last time Piccolo saw her, Lauren and the boy with a demon tattoo crept in the backseat of a black Mustang with tinted windows.

Piccolo kicked angrily at loose rocks on the pavement. She glanced again at her giggling, now intoxicated friend Paige and the parked car where Lauren had escaped to and felt more and more like the baby they had called her. *What was the point of going through all the trouble of sneaking out if you weren't even going to have fun?* Piccolo accepted a red plastic cup from a muscular skyscraper of a boy in black leather. She smiled thanks at the tall guy in black and nearly dropped her cup when she stared into his eyes, two glowing orbs the color of sulfur. She blinked and saw black shades instead. Piccolo laughed at herself and took two careful sips. By her fourth sip, she pushed herself off of Lauren's car and danced over to the wildly gyrating teens. The music boomed louder.

Piccolo closed her eyes and rocked back and forth to the music. A couple pressed in against her. She playfully tried to push back against them but found them immovable and…. strong. Rough, cold hands slipped around her waist and groped the tender area beneath the small of her back and her delicate, flat stomach under her belted pants! Her body went rigid and cold in panic. When Piccolo blinked her eyes open, she found all around her teens frozen in movement like statues. She saw dancing teens stationary, their arms, hips, and legs frozen in mid-sway. Groups of teens held curious, stiff poses, their cups held unmoving to their lips. Others' lips locked in perpetual smiles and kisses, and still more had their mouths open in mid-laugh or sentence.

Paige and her pimply consort held a frozen, casual embrace. Only the music had not stopped blaring and grew louder. There were also red stains in various places, splattered on the ground, splashed against cars and trucks. The final dregs of her inebriation wore off in a rising panic. Without knowing why, Piccolo rubbed her back and stomach. Her skin stung there as if it had been burned.

As Piccolo looked around the lot in a wild panic, her eyes caught glimpse of a beautiful pale green couple in black leather with glowing sulfur eyes and long black hair. Piccolo realized that the male had been the one who had given her the strong drink earlier and that now they had been watching her and found her panic entertaining. They each wore the same evil smile as if they both shared a delicious secret. The more she watched the pair, the more she realized how difficult it was to take her eyes off of them. They were impossibly beautiful with long, flowing black hair and sensual lips. They also radiated danger. They looked more like sister and brother but held each other as if they were more intimate … lovers.

The scantily-clad, green woman parted her lips and a forked black tongue darted and flitted between them. She waved her hand, motioning for someone or something else to join them. The brother brushed elegant, thin fingers with polished ruby talons along the back of what looked like a wrinkled, hairless dog. It shook its leg in ecstasy. As Piccolo looked closer in shocked silence, she realized that the dog wasn't really a dog at all, but what looked like a mutated ghoul on hunches. Its face looked like the skull of a monster with corpse-like skin stretched across it. Its bulging, pupil-less eyes had no lids, and stared unblinking at its prey. The eyes were completely black except in cases when it was excited. Then they glowed red. And where a nose should have been, mere slits seemed carved into its ghoulish face. The hell hound raised a hind leg with fingerlike toes and dagger talons to scratch the back of its neck. It licked the brother's fingers and stiffened at a sound in the distance.

An ice cream truck with peculiar symbols moved toward them, advancing slowly like a predator stalking its prey. Piccolo didn't notice the Beast with monstrous claws and rows of sharp teeth before the hell hounds lunged for her, snapping their jaws and growling deeply. She heard a dry, voice laugh that was pure evil.

"I am winning, Noble," It said. "The Blood of Seven shall be mine!"

Piccolo screamed.

5

Time for Confessions

N oble passed the night in fitful restlessness punctuated by nightmares, nearly missing his bus the next morning. He remembered dreaming of Piccolo, Lark's best friend as she cried and screamed. He felt her overwhelming fear and a burning sensation on his back and stomach. He dreamed of a monster that resembled a ghoulish Gollum of *Lord of the Rings* and behaved like a dog. Noble didn't think that a creature could be more disturbing than Gollum, but there it was snapping at Piccolo in his dreams. What disturbed him most was the voice. It addressed him by his name this time. *I am winning, Noble. The Blood of Seven shall be mine!* Noble shuddered.

Noble threw back the covers and sat up. The movement left his head spinning and dizzy. His head wobbled heavily on his neck and his brow pounded in a dull headache. Noble didn't know if he was coming down with something or if he was suffering from a mild shock from yesterday's events.

Full of questions from yesterday's Trial and attack, Noble frowned at not being able to talk to his mother about her doubtful testimony, the creepy summons, his family's service to the Light, or the graceful janitor Abe. Why had his mother spoken against him? Why had she, his sister Lark, and even his best friend, kept this information from him or warned him about his Trial or Training? But hadn't Abe warned Noble not to discuss his Trial or Training with anyone, especially not his mother? Who could he trust to talk about his fear of failing or of dying or of letting his mother down?

To the death. That is what the hooded figure at the Trial had charged him to, and he had, without question or complaint, accepted the oath. As he hurried downstairs, he noticed that his mother had left a breakfast of fresh strawberries, melon, maple sausages, and hot, homemade cinnamon buns. He wrapped up his breakfast to eat on the way to the bus stop and looked around for his mother and sister. His mother had already left for school, and he heard Lark rustling about in her room.

"Come on, Phony!" he yelled. He knew the nickname annoyed her, so he yelled it at the top of his lungs. "*Phooooooooneeeeeee!*"

As he waited out front, he heard Lark's thunderous descent down the stairs. She slammed the front door, locked it, and hurried to join him out front.

"Okay, Okay," she snapped. "Keep your boxers on! Why do you insist on calling me that god-awful name?" He walked up the path ahead of her, fuming at Nick and her betrayal.

"Why didn't you tell me about my Trial and Luminaries?" he fired back. To his mild shock, Lark was quiet. Noticing her pained expression, he pressed further. "Why didn't you tell me or at least warn me? Phony I – I could have died! Why -"

"Nobby, I couldn't. I couldn't tell you. Momma, Daddy, Nick, we were all forbidden to tell you to protect you. To give you a fighting chance at surviving—"

"Surviving?" Noble said with a derisive snort. "Is that what you call pitting me against freaky, killer cock roaches and giant fists of furye?"

"We didn't tell you to protect you. All children of Luminaries are kept ignorant of who they are and their powers to keep the Darkness from killing them before their time. The Darkness reads minds and visits your dreams. It sends out its agents to kill you. It is common practice to keep the fledgling Lightworker ignorant until his mentor teaches him how to guard his thoughts and emotions. Otherwise, you would be slaughtered. Your destiny in the Light is so great that the Darkness has killed and tortured many to find you and others like you. Even those close to you. It's dangerous! Daddy tried to plan for your training before he left, leaving us a set of core values to steer us on the right—the right path," Lark broke off. Her eyes brimmed with tears whenever she mentioned their father. Like Noble, his father's absence was hard on her, too. She sniffled and wiped the tears from her cheeks and continued.

"Momma has been beside herself with worry," she said. "She's been so scared of losing you before your Trial."

Noble walked on, silenced by his sister's words. He tried to steer the conversation from talk of their father.

"So when was your Trial?" he asked after some moments. "Were you attacked by killer roaches, too?"

"I had my Trial when I was eight," Lark answered. "And everyone's trial is different. My Trial wasn't nearly as dangerous. I had to sing my way through hives of killer bees. As long as I sang, they were mesmerized and dull and didn't attack me. I had Momma and Aunt Regalia to help me. You are a Light Warrior and Salvation's Champion. I am a Handmaiden of Light. I use my gifts for healing, peacemaking, discernment, and encouraging. I am called to assist you and even fight at your side, but your task is yours and yours alone.

'I had Momma and Aunt Regalia to help me,' Lark said.. Why wasn't Momma or Auntie Regalia around to help me? Noble wondered. This business with the Light and the Dark was confusing.

"What about Nick?" Noble asked. "Is he a Light Warrior, too?"

"Yes," Lark answered. "He is also a Light Warrior, but not a Champion. He can also fight against the Darkness and aid you in your fight, but his assignment is different from yours. This is a big fight, and it is fought on several fronts. That is why each Luminary is born and trained for a specific purpose. Nick had his Trial last year. Remember his chicken pox?"

Noble nodded. Nick had been away for over a month, and when he returned he showed no scars to mark him as one who had suffered from chicken pox. Noble had never questioned it. Noble began to understand that his was a family of secrets, but they were kept to protect others, not to hurt them.

As they rounded the bend, he found Nick waiting for them. Nick stared down at his feet and kicked at a pine comb. He stole several glances at Noble and appeared guilty and troubled. He looked up hastily and stared from Lark to Noble and back to Lark again.

"It's alright, Nick," Lark said.

Nick looked relieved. He ran over to them and fell into step beside Noble. After an awkward silence, he spoke.

"I'm sorry, Man," Nick said. "Look, I wanted to tell you, but I promised your dad and your mom, Miss Genesis, that I wouldn't tell. Besides, I couldn't lose my best bud, too."

Noble was touched by Nick's frankness. Nick said he didn't want to lose his best bud, *too*. Noble knew he spoke in reference to his deceased mother, killed when he was a baby. Nick rarely spoke about her death.

"It's okay," Noble said. "You promised my parents, and now I understand that knowing about who I was too soon would have put me in peril. I guess you have nothing to be sorry for." Noble forgave them all, but the betrayal still rankled in the back of his mind.

Nick smiled. Dimples creased his chocolate cheeks, and his wide grin was almost as dazzling as the straight, white teeth of his toothsome smile. Noble smiled back at him. He couldn't stay mad at Nick for long.

"We start Training. Phony and I get to train with you," Nick said. "From this point on, we're in it together."

Noble didn't feel reassured by Nick's words. *How exactly can I save Salvation and fight the Darkness alone?* They boarded the bus and rode in silence.

6

The Darkness Attacks

Very little about school was educational, encouraging, or safe. In fact, Noble likened high school to the menacing wilds of *Animal Planet*. Bigger, older teens leered behind lockers or skulked in the hallways, ready to pounce on the weak or the feeble. Even the adults were immune to the violence or viciousness meted out by criminals in training.

A gaggle of long-legged, skittish teen girls crowded in amongst each other for safety, and of course, gossip. As Noble passed the flock of girls, they snapped up their long necks in a wary alertness. Once they regarded him as non-threatening, or worse, unworthy of their notice, they resumed their chatter. A few of the girls' glances lingered, eyeing him in open curiosity. A jock with more shoulders and chest that could be placed into a teenaged body, a member of Ray's entourage, called out to Noble. A timid freshman with glasses steered a wide path away from the group of boys. One of the entourage noticed his escape and pushed him into the wall of lockers.

"Hey, it's the Snitch," the jock yelled at Noble.

"Douche," yelled another. The rest of the jungle jeered and howled in cruel laughter. Noble felt more and more like prey, a startled deer, not frightened but helpless, before a pacing pack of predators. The freshmen scrambled to his feet and hurried away from the crowd as the gang closed in around Noble, blocking his escape.

"I heard you got beat down like a punk," the jock said.

"Like a punk snitch," another gang member yelled. The two of them pressed in even closer to Noble, their chests and bodies nearly touching. Noble noticed that the jock quivered in menacing violence. As he stared at him, waves of evil intent reverberated from his muscular being, his flared nostrils, and most of all, his hard, unmerciful eyes. He wasn't as huge as Ray, but he was large enough. A gang member behind Noble nudged him roughly. Noble stumbled a few steps forward, caught himself from falling, pulled himself up erect, and stood his ground, facing the jock squarely.

"You need to get your eyes checked because that's not what happened," Noble said. As Noble spoke, the jock and four other teens moved closer still. Noble hadn't been this close to a crowd of people since the family reunion when aunts, uncles, and cousins pressed in around him in a loving embrace. Noble did not sense the same feelings of love.

"It was you, alright," the jock said. "I heard you cried like a baby and begged for your mommy". The crowd and the gang laughed harder. Emboldened by the laughing crowd, the jock continued. "She couldn't help you because she was busy selling fish on the corner. I can smell her now."

Noble didn't realize that he had closed the last few inches of space between him and the jock. If Noble sneezed, their noses would have touched. Without knowing, Noble clinched and unclenched his fists. Staring directly into the large, oily pores around the jock's nose, he fought a compulsion to punch the jock in his face.

Noble could take the taunts about himself easily. Really, the jock and the rest of Ray's gang weren't that original. The moment the comments turned to insults about his mother, he felt a powerful maelstrom whirling inside of him. Remembering the way the gang attacked him the other day, he imagined knocking the jock's gold teeth down his throat. He could actually feel his knuckles crack and fingers jam, connecting with the jock's lips, oily nose, gums, and teeth. He heard, felt the crunch of bone, of teeth and flesh and saw the jock's head fly back with the impact. Warm blood coated his fingers... *No!* This was not him.

Noble never felt such violence and anger before, not even when the gang attacked him on the bus ramp days ago. It was scary and powerful, like the eye of a malignant hurricane. And he didn't like it.

Always one to rush to Noble's aid, Nick responded. Blowing on a whistle attached to his key chain, he made his way through the throng.

"Disperse! Disperse!" he yelled gruffly.

Nick cleared his throat and pulled up his belted slacks to just beneath his chest, the hem of his pants just skirting his ankles. More students snickered. His signature dimples creased his coffee colored skin and his long lashes winked over intense, dark brown eyes. Noble stared back at him with piercing hazel ones.

"Wash your mouth, wash your mouth, young man!" Nick yelled. "This has nothing to do with *your* mom's lack of personal hygiene, although you may want to ask her to schedule *you* a visit to the dentist. What do you brush your teeth with? Cheetos?"

For effect, Nick pushed up an imaginary pair of glasses over his nose, exaggerating the gesture so that the crowd of students would notice. They did. The hallway exploded into guffaws and jeers. The gang of jocks hung back in confusion. Not given to thinking quickly, the jock folded his muscular arms over his broad chest and blew large puffs of air out of his mouth in frustration. This only made the students laugh louder.

Mr. Crandall, the school principal, rushed into the throng of students, blowing on his whistle. His powder blue, polyester slacks belted millimeters beneath his chest and skirting the tops of his ankles, revealed thick, striped tube socks stuffed into loafers.

"Disperse! Disperse!" he yelled, pushing up his real, tortoise shell-rimmed glasses on his nose. "And wash your mouths!" The crowd laughed even louder.

"Anybody caught being tardy to class starts of the year with a detention. Now get to class!" Mr. Crandall said.

The jungle of students dissipated into smaller groups, migrating to their new classes. Nick fell into step beside Noble.

"Man with your impressive SAT vocabulary, you'd think you would be able to crack back on those morons who insult you," Nick said tentatively. He knew this was a touchy subject, and one that Noble did not like to talk about.

Noble shrugged in irritable silence. He hated that once again, Nick had come to his rescue, and that once again, Nick was right. He *should've* stood up to those Cro-Magnon idiots, but that would actually be a step up for the Neanderthals they really were. But as extensive as Noble's vocabulary was, he did not know how to crack or check or whatever it was kids his age did to tear others down with their hurtful insults. He'd been on the receiving end of insults too many times, and it wasn't as if he was scared of the rest of the kids, at least not most of them, but something within him held him back. He didn't want to explode one day from holding all of the anger in. He'd have to do something and soon.

Nick made cracking on others seem like an art form. He could insult others with ease, employing an innate ability that was as unique as it was creative, and at times even poetic. But that wasn't why they were best friends since kindergarten. He could probably even fight back if hadn't been instilled in him to choose his battles wisely and to fight with his words, not with his hands.

Many times, Nick's mouth got him into a lot of trouble and more fights than Noble could count with boys who with more adept with their fists than with their words. And even though Nick wasn't part of the in-crowd, especially because of his second hand clothes and the repeating home drama of abuse from his grandfather, he was undeniably the class clown. The students could not help but laugh at Nick's antics. Secretly, Noble knew that Nick laughed to keep from crying. Laughter masked the hurt caused by an absent father, his deceased mother, whom he adored, and an alcoholic, often abusive grandfather. If he listened to Nick closely, Noble could hear the crying beneath the tears. And Nick laughed a lot.

They continued their walk in an uneasy silence, although Noble and Nick had an easy friendship that could withstand the lapses in silences. They understood each other so well that words weren't even necessary most times.

Nick left Noble to his private thoughts, and Noble was grateful for the gesture. Since the unbelievable acceptance of his Trial, his acceptance of the task to be the Lightworker and inducted into a secret society that fought supernatural evil, Noble had been unable to sleep well most nights and was plagued by disturbing nightmares when he could sleep. Most days he was given to fits of irritable moodiness. Nick, who Noble had learned was also a part of the society as well as his sister and entire family, understood his moods, too, and supported him. They were great friends, almost like brothers. To Noble and his family, they were brothers, and that was all there was to it.

They were almost near homeroom class, and because of their brisk pace they could enjoy a few moments of free time to play a few minutes of Zombie Smash on Noble's Nintendo DS or perhaps even to look over Noble's biology notes before first period. However, Noble was seized by a deep feeling of foreboding. He noticed the familiar dip in temperature, a shimmering in the fabric of reality, a rustling and roiling of the molecules in the air. The light in the hallway dimmed and dark shadows, a growing wave of whispers and claws and teeth, raced upon the walls, ceiling and floors, hovering and advancing towards them with deadly purpose.

Noble felt a peculiar sensation in his stomach and chest, a tightening, a physical reaction to intense danger. The skin on the back of his neck and behind his ears tingled and chill bumps erupted on his arms.

Noble stopped in caution and Nick crept behind him in a wary second. He thought he heard angry voices that whispered and called out to him.

I come for you. I sense you. I taste your fear. Give up. Give up or die. I will tear your flesh from your bones.

Noble's heart thundered in his chest and he was just about to run grabbing Nick behind him when he saw a bright light piercing and swallowing up the cold, angry darkness and its menacing whispers. It was Mr. Cedarian, or Abe as Noble and Nick called him. A strong light emanated from his outstretched right hand and gobbled up the blackness and shadow. It restored the temperature and returned the lighting to normal. The hallway appeared like it did on any ordinary day, and for a moment, Noble wondered if he had imagined it all. He glanced at Nick whose breathing was rapid and knew that he had felt and seen and heard the Darkness, too. When the danger seemed to have abated, Abe stood in front of the boys and clapped his strong earthen hands together loudly. It sounded like a clap of thunder, but Noble knew he had not heard of a chance of rain storms today. And then he knew, as Abe had told him before, his Training would soon commence.

7

Training

Before Noble could blink, the boys were in Abe's ornate, comfortable office. Abe moved toward his grandfather clock and opened the window that covered the face of the time piece. Abe stretched his arms wide and his large, earth-colored hands exuded shimmering, golden strands between them. He gathered up the shimmering, golden band between outstretched hands. Noble thought that it looked and moved like the cool, corn silk his mother made him remove when he shucked corn for Sunday dinner. As Noble looked, the shimmering band floated in the air like a Portuguese Man of War floated in the deep or a breeze rippling beneath a curtain.

"This is time," Abe told the boys. His eyes twinkled with excitement and wonder like a toddler who had just seen his first Christmas tree light up. "It's not a fixed line but in fact coils and reverberates and loops back upon itself. For brief periods, a select few Luminaries, and servants of the Darkness, can manipulate it. They can stop it or travel backward and forwards in it. I've stopped time for our first lesson." Noble and Nick stared at each other in awe. It was never a boring moment in Abe's company.

"Wow, that is amazing," a voice, a familiar voice said behind him. He turned around to see Lark twirling a tendril of her curly hair.

"It is rather prodigious, Mr. Abe," Noble admitted. In response to his comment, he heard several responses of sucked teeth. Noble's smile faded as he walked out of the sitting room to Mr. Abe's study. Behind two short bookcases seated in two winged-back chairs sat his god-brother and god-sister, Tenebrous and Stone, the children of his creeper godfather, Cedar Judas Bane. Noble could not understand why his mother held Mr. Bane in any kind of regard. It was just plain creepy the way Mr. Bane stared at her, trailing Genesis' every move with his eyes. His father never spoke of it, but Noble knew he didn't like the man either. His mother was a creature of extreme devotion to her friends and family, kind hearted and loving. It was why so many people loved her and why he and his family adored her, but still, there was something not right with Mr. Bane. His god-brother and god-sister teased and insulted Lark and him at every available opportunity.

"'It is rather prodigious'", Tenebrous mimicked. "If it isn't Dorky the SAT wonder geek and his annoying sister". Tenebrous was the only guy that he knew that wore fresh pressed jeans with razor sharp creases. His legs were crossed casually in front of him while he laced his fingers together on his lap. He looked down his nose in a perpetual sneer. Stone, who sat filing her French manicured nails and flipping through the latest copy of *Teen* magazine across from her brother, rolled her dark brown eyes and snickered at his comment.

"If you picked up a book or two once in a while, you'd know a few SAT words, too," Noble said. "In case you haven't noticed, not everyone holds monosyllabic conversations."

"Oh, you mean like loser and prick-face?" Tenebrous asked.

"That's two syllables, *Tinny*," Noble said. "Try boob and ass. Go look up those. They suit you perfectly." Just then, Nick came into the room and threw his hands in the air in mock disgust when he saw them.

"Awwh Man! The Adams Family is here?" he said. "I think I'm gonna' be sick!"

"You're already sick," Tenebrous said. He seemed even more excited by Nick's presence. Noble braced himself for Tenebrous' comments, for he knew him to be excessively cruel and hurtful.

"The apple doesn't fall far from the tree," Tenebrous said smiling. "Let's see, with a crack-head, homosexual convict for a father, an alcoholic for a grandfather, and a nut-case mother who was murdered, you're as good as crazy *and dead*, anyway---"

Before Tenebrous finished his sentence, Nick lunged for him sending the chair toppling backwards. Mr. Abe flashed into the room, his body appearing before them as quickly as lightning zigzagged across the sky. He walked over to the fighting boys as currents of wind ripped around him.

"Enough!" he yelled. At his words the two boys froze, like fierce and angry statues: Nick's hands were locked around Tenebrous' throat, and Tenebrous' hands clung to Nick's fingers, trying without success to pry open his tight grasp. Tenebrous' eyes were stretched wide in shock. Nick's face was a picture of frozen fury.

"Now is not the time for petty rivalries and trivial disputes!" Abe yelled. "Nor is it the time for unwarranted cruelty!" He spoke meaningfully at Tenebrous as he cowered under Abe's fiery stare. Abe's voice filled the room, and a wild wind toppled the books off the shelves, ripped away the post cards from the walls, and whipped and lashed out at the curtains. As his voice grew louder, Abe's form grew taller and bigger, and fury flashed like lightning from his eyes.

"The Darkness uses anger, hurt, and manipulations to divide us, to conquer us before we even begin our quest. Put this fighting and malice behind you before they give way to footholds for the Enemy! Then all will be lost and we all perish. If you can't stop this fighting, I can put you both away myself, and I promise you, you won't like the outcome." No one in the room dared to move or even breathe in Abe's powerful rage.

The boys were set free from their temporary, unmoving prison and fell to the ground. They looked with wild anger at each other, but after glancing at Abe's giant form, forced their breathing to normal and made themselves calm down.

"I do not mean to yell at you," Abe said, his voice returning to its soft-spoken elegance and his huge form shrank back to its normal six feet six inches. "But all we have in this fight against a vicious, murderous enemy is each other. We must get along, but more than that we must learn to trust one another with our very lives. This animosity must cease." Abe walked over to both boys and placed his huge palms on their foreheads. The moment he touched them, they shrank back closing their eyes.

"Understanding," Abe said. Their eyes flickered back and forth beneath closed eyelids as if they were watching a movie or perhaps having a dream.

"Compassion," Abe said. Noble, Lark, and Stone watched as tears dropped from the corners of both of their eyes. Tenebrous wiped away his tears with quick, rough hands. Even with his eyes closed, Noble could sense that Tenebrous was embarrassed by his tears. Nick cried unabashedly, the silent tears streamed freely and gave him release.

"Peace," Abe said and whispered words that only they could hear. They both opened their eyes and faced each other, and to Noble's surprise, shook hands. They each retreated to a side of the room and waited in silence. Moved by Abe's words and more significantly by Tenebrous and Nick's actions, he walked to the middle of the study and spoke.

"I'm sorry, Abe," he said, "And Nick and Tenebrous. I've disrespected you and disgraced our efforts and our cause. I will not bring confusion and dishonor to our group, our family again. Forgive me, and let me make amends."

Mr. Abe smiled and patted Noble on the shoulder.

"I accept your apology," Abe said. He walked over to Tenebrous and Nick and shook each one's hand in turn. "I am proud of your willingness to humble yourselves and make peace." He walked over to Tenebrous' back pack and putting on a pair of protective gloves from his desk drawer, plucked a huge, black tic-like creature from the fabric. Once discovered, the tick fluttered its wings, buzzed angrily, and wriggled to escape, but Abe held him fast between his large, powerful hands. He opened his other palm to emit a blue flame. The tic shook and squealed. "Someone's been very busy," Abe said. He ignited the evil tick into burning, azure flames. It turned to a foul-smelling ash. Noble ran to open the study window. Strangely, a gentle breeze from inside the room lifted the ashes and carried them to the window. The breeze dispersed the ashes and carried them out of the window, where a larger breeze whisked them away from this domain.

"Thank you, Cleansing Spirit." Abe said.

"You are most welcome, Wise One," a light, feminine voice whispered in the retreating wind. All was silent.

Who was Abe talking to? Noble wanted to ask. Abe smiled at Noble and winked. But with all of the drama that had just transpired, he thought better of it.

"Wise choice," Abram said so quietly that Noble was surprised that he could hear him. "Perhaps later."

"That was a rioting tick. It lodged itself onto Tenebrous' back pack and caused the confusion that you saw today. It is a lower level demon and is not developed enough to spy for the Enemy until it feeds on discord, fighting, and anger. Had we not quelled the fray between us today, it would have grown and given away our location and any traits about us that the Usurper could use against us. It's important to note, however, that it cannot attack unless we give in to our anger. We must always be vigilant and cautious. This is war, young Luminaries. Take care that you do not forget."

Noble and the rest of them nodded their heads in wary agreement. Abe smiled at the two of them and his deep, clear brown eyes seemed to light up his expression, making him look younger than his years. Just how old was Mr. Cedarian? And who was this man? Noble did not know. He got the feeling that he had been around for a long time. Abe smiled again at Noble, and Noble got the impression that Abe read his thoughts. In fact, he knew he could read his mind since before the Trial he had shared conversations with him without speaking a word. But he spoke to the unlikely group today.

"Okay Children," Abe said.

"Good morning, Mr. Abe," they all responded in unison, some in earnest and some as if they would rather be somewhere else. Noble's heart beat again for he was excited to learn from his wise old friend.

"What kind of janitor has an office with furnishings more refined than its principal?" Tenebrous asked over his familiar scornful expression. Noble knew that many of the girls at school regarded Tenebrous as handsome, and maybe he would be if he didn't look down his nose at everyone all the times and wear that ridiculous sneer.

Noble stared over at Tenebrous, and was not surprised that the others including his sister joined him. Would he never learn? But Noble noticed that Abe offered him a patient smile.

"You should never judge a person by his work or his color or his beliefs," he responded. "You judge a man by his character and his actions. I'm here at this school because I have a vested interest in it and its students. We have for generations. And let me remind you that my wealth is also none of your concern, young Bane. The reason we are here is to prepare ourselves for battle and to arm ourselves against the Darkness and to sharpen your skills and utilize your gifts."

Noble warily conceded that Mr. Cedarian spoke and behaved in a manner that was used to money, old money, but he was the kind of person who did not regard people as important because they had it. Noble found another reason to like Mr. Abe.

Mr. Abe smiled again. "Today we work on seeing into the hearts of men, reading their expressions or their intentions. Often we don't know why people behave the way they do, and if we understood them more, we could see more clearly to help them, to lead them to the Light," he said.

Lark continued to twirl her hair around her finger. She looked at Mr. Abe with a mixture of unmasked curiosity and admiration. He smiled at her, too. She smiled back, her eyes were the same startling hazel-amber color as her brother.

Stone was a dark beauty who had recently cut her waist length hair, to the chagrin of her mother, in a severe bob. It actually enhanced her beauty, accentuating her high cheek bones and opulent mahogany skin. She rolled her eyes at Mr. Abe's words and especially his kind gesture to Lark, who she could not stand. Noble was wary of her, and not just because of her beauty either. He'd seen her throw her older and larger brother Tenebrous over on his back using both her physical and mental strengths. He gave her a wide berth and a well-earned respect. Mr. Abe smiled at her, too.

Abe spoke again, "I want you to close your eyes and clear your minds. Empty them of any distracting thoughts, any upsetting emotions. The enemy uses emotions against you, so guard your minds and try to keep your hearts and your intentions pure."

Noble closed his eyes, trying to empty them of the mounting fear he felt since his father had gone missing, his expectations of him and his Trial, his worry about his mother, the embarrassing situation that happened before homeroom today, and even the frightening shadows. He slowed his breathing and stared in amazement when Mr. Abe placed an image of an emptying basin of water in his mind.

"All of your troubles are draining away," he said.

The other teens gasped in amazement, too.

"All that I do, you will soon learn to do, too," he continued. As soon as he cleared their minds by placing an image of the emptying basin, he replaced that image with the scene of Noble's teasing today. Lark gasped in horror at the muscular jock who loomed over her brother and Tenebrous laughed, showing his sneer again.

"I thought we were to empty our minds of distressing thoughts," Noble said. He regarded Tenebrous with open hostility, trying to remember his promise for peace. Surprisingly, Stone remained neutral.

56

"Patience, young Noble," Mr. Abe said. "You will soon see the reason for this painful memory. I apologize for the intrusion, but we will all learn from you today."

What could they learn from this situation, Noble pondered? That he was a dork or worse as the jock had called him?

"The Dark preys on emotions, feeds on them, escalates fear, and breeds confusion and brouhahas," he said. "However, I want you to look at the young man who is hurling insults. Look deep within your hearts and minds. Tell me what you see."

Noble pressed his lips together firmly in concentration and tried to shake his embarrassment. He focused on the jock. As he looked he gasped again when he noticed a small demon, what looked like a mud-colored imp, ugly and hairy, resting on the shoulders on the young man who had insulted him. Its grimy hands held the jock's temples as if it were holding a prize. As Noble looked deeper, he noticed the young man's discomfort. He felt his headache, probably from the demon, and he saw a memory play out in front of him. The young man clinched his fists as he watched his mother's newest boyfriend beat her with his fists. He tried to fight the older man, who was intoxicated, but impossibly stronger and bigger than the jock. The alcoholic smacked him in the mouth. Noble tasted the jock's blood, felt the pain of the blow, but most of all felt the pain of the young man who felt helpless as he watched his mother.

Noble wiped away tears. He did not need to see to know that his sister Lark was crying, too. Stone remained silent but very thoughtful. Surprisingly, Tenebrous did not comment at all. Noble realized he did not see the image but tried to hide it from the others. Nick was also curiously silent, and then Noble knew that Nick was having a few flashbacks of his own, as his own mother was killed violently by his father. Noble didn't know exactly. He reached over and tapped Nick's shoulder. Nick shook his head, and Noble could tell he did not want the others to know, so he let his arm fall to his side and remained silent.

And as he looked in the painful memory of himself, he felt some remorse for the young jock who had teased him. Noble also saw that light emanated from his hands in the image. Power surged from his hands, and he knew now why he resisted in fighting. He could kill someone.

Noble was shocked by this fact most of all, and he would have paused to consider his rapid thoughts, but to the surprise of most of them the demon, in the middle of the memory that played before him, focused his eyes away from his victim, glared menacingly at Noble, and hissed. Abe clapped his hands again, but Noble struck out first. He sent a surge of raw energy that reduced the demon to a pile of dust.

Mr. Abram replaced the image with the emptying basin of water again. Noble's pulse and breathing returned to normal.

"There is much we have learned today children," Abe said. "Who would like to explain?"

Lark answered first. She was the first to raise her hand in all her classes and many students hated her for it. She was beautiful and intelligent, but most of all, she was a "goody-two-shoes" and that seemed to irk most of the girls. She was still quite popular, though.

"We learned that we don't know why man responds in brutish behavior and that perhaps he is literally carrying demons," Lark said. "I think we need to have a sensitivity to understand others so that we can lead them to the Light."

"Precisely, Miss Lark," Mr. Abe beamed at her.

"Know your enemy," Stone responded. "Or at least know what he's struggling with so you know how to respond."

"Very insightful, Miss Stone," Mr. Abe said. "Anyone else?" he asked the others.

Nick shook his head silently and Tenebrous sulked instead of sneered. But Noble also remained silent musing over the images and surprised by his display of power and the demon who could see him.

"Mr. Abe?" Noble asked. "Were we attacked, in the hallway this morning?

"Yes, you were," Mr. Abe said. "I will not always be there so I am showing you as much as I can so you can arm yourselves. I want you to take a 30 minute break before I return you to normal time. Remember the rules. Tell no one of our work here or our lessons. Understand?"

"Yes, Mr. Abe," they all said in unison.

Mr. Abe clapped his hands again and Noble found himself and Nick outside of class right after Mr. Abe had dispersed the shadows. He was sure that Lark and the others were exactly where they were before the attack, too. He followed Nick into the class silently. Noble was scared.

Before Noble entered the class, he noticed a poster of a shy, pretty girl with sparkling brown eyes and a pretty smile. Noble leaned in closer to get a better look. She was Piccolo, Lark's best friend who sat with her on the bus, shopped with her at the mall after school, and slept over often on weekends. She was the hysterical girl who was being chased by the creatures in his latest dream. She was also missing, the latest kidnapping victim. As soon as he realized who she was he felt Lark's anguish and despair before he heard her scream. He felt an intense sadness unlike any he'd ever experienced and sought to comfort his sister. Noble realized that Piccolo's captors were not serial killers, or kidnappers who demanded ransom. They were a malignant force that was pure, unadulterated evil. And Noble had to defeat it…. alone.

8

Piccolo's Prayer Vigil

Noble dragged his heels and kicked at small gray stones that lined the church parking lot as he followed his mother and Lark up the path to the church. His mother Genesis pulled herself up into the full five feet 7 inches of her frame and carefully neatened the tasseled hem of her ornate, black, silk skirt. She waved hello to the young Mr. Simmons, the young math teacher, and kissed the cheek of his newly wed wife who unbeknownst to others glowed in the first days of pregnancy.

"Congratulations," Genesis whispered in Mrs. Simmons' ear.

"How did you know?" Mrs. Simmons asked, blushing and hugging Genesis back.

"I dreamed of your son's coming the night before Mr. Simmons introduced you," Genesis said with a sad smile. "I thought it was prudent of me to wait until after your marriage and pregnancy before telling you. You have many years ahead of you as a family. You will be a great mother." Mrs. Simons hugged Genesis even tighter, breathless with the news of her good fortune in her embrace.

"Thank you, Miss Genesis," she said. And then her bright eyes turned serious and melancholy. Her pretty forehead creased with worry in her sepia, heart-shaped face. "I can't believe our Piccolo is missing. Deacon and Mrs. Thomas must be beside themselves with worry."

Noble saw his mother's clear, hazel eyes echo the same sadness and fear as Mrs. Simmons.

"This is a frightening time for us all," Genesis said. "I'm going to give these to Mrs. Thomas before the prayer vigil starts." She patted the contents of a blue bag that hung on her shoulder.

"Are those your banana nut muffins?" Mr. Simmons asked turning away from a conversation he was having with another church member on the steps of the church. He followed his nose to Genesis' bag.

"Go ahead and take one, William," she said. "They're still warm, just like you like them."

As the three of them moved on, they noticed the elder mothers, ancient Mrs. Dobbs and even more ancient Mrs. Grubbs. Noble fell back as they each gave dry pecks on his mother and sister's cheeks. They poked and prodded on Lark's thighs and hips, while she submitted with a practiced calm and patience. Noble thought the sisters reminded him of the witches of *MacBeth*.

"There's only two of us," Mrs. Dobbs said grinning wickedly at Noble. "There are *three* witches in *MacBeth*."

Noble would have been alarmed by the old woman's comments, except that he was used to the all-to-peculiar coincidences of the elder mothers' ability to comment on his thoughts. He stopped trying to figure them out long ago.

"That girl sure is growing."

"Look at those hips, Genesis. Those are good breedin' hips."

"She courtin' yet?"

"You better keep your shot gun handy."

The oldest sister cackled as she poked and prodded Lark's hips with a surprisingly strong, bony finger. To this latest injustice, Lark found

Genesis' hand, squeezed it, and pulled on her mother none-too-discretely to leave the ancient sisters behind.

"Good to see you, Mother Dobbs. Mother Grubbs," Genesis said as she walked up the stairs and into the church. Lark followed behind, walking away as quickly as two inch heels could carry her with the practiced caution and grace of one used to walking in heels.

Noble dragged behind his sister and mother as they made the "rounds", greeting Brother Eldred, Deacon Voyles, The Wilson and Jenkins families, each with kids who looked just as miserable as Noble, and others. He couldn't help but notice that Genesis made nearly imperceptible nods to certain members, certain members he was sure must have been secret members of the community of Light. His hunch was confirmed when she made eye contact with Mr. Abe. They both nodded as they passed one another. Mr. Abe smiled briefly and warmly at Noble and Lark. Noble noticed that Mr. Abe gave the same warm yet brief smile to everyone he met. Somehow, Noble knew that this was not the right time to ask Mr. Abe about the others in the Light. So he focused on his sister.

Noble cast a sideways glance at Lark, who looked inconsolable and unreachable with drooping shoulders and a silent, cast down stare. He used his mind to probe her world of melancholy:

> *If only I had been there....*
> *If only I could've warned her somehow...*
> *I thought I was protecting her by avoiding her, by not telling her about the*
> *Darkness.... I should've known she'd be more vulnerable without me...*
> *If only I had been there...*
> *If only....*

Her train of guilty thoughts repeated themselves. Noble pulled away from her mind, but not before feeling a crushing wave of sadness and despair. He glanced again at Lark. Her eyes were swollen and puffy and marked by dark rings. Since learning of the news of Piccolo's disappearance she cried all night without sleeping. Her nose was red and shiny, and silent tears still fell from her eyes. And yet these changes did not mar her beauty.

Genesis stopped before Mr. and Mrs. Thomas. Noble and Lark stood behind her. Mr. Thomas, in his fifties and beginning to bald, sat with his shoulders slumped in the front pew. He draped his arm protectively around his wife, Mrs. Thomas, a stately woman of aged beauty. It was easy to see where Piccolo got her looks. Mrs. Thomas wringed her manicured hands in despair.

Genesis leaned down and patted Mr. Thomas on the shoulder and hugged Mrs. Thomas tightly, an embrace that communicated a timeless, silent empathy between all mothers, especially when one mother has lost one of her own. Noble felt and saw the warmth that passed from his mother into Mrs. Thomas. It was invisible to others, but not to him, a glowing warmth. Genesis parted slowly, gently, and whispered in Mrs. Thomas' ear.

Noble noticed that whatever his mother said to Mrs. Thomas seemed to give her comfort, and Mrs. Thomas accepted Genesis' gift with quiet dignity and with something else…. hope. Genesis shepherded Noble and Lark in the pews three rows behind the Thomases, but not before the Thomases grabbed Noble. With weary and frantic countenances, they spoke to him.

"We believe in you young Light Warrior," Mr. Thomas said.

"We know you will bring our beloved Piccolo home and the other innocents, too," Mrs. Thomas said. Her tearful eyes still shone with the hope Genesis inspired.

Noble stumbled under the weight of their expectations. *What could he do? How could he actually help them? Rescue Piccolo? What if he wasn't strong enough? What if he wasn't ready?* Noble heard an evil voice chuckle with glee in his mind. Immediately after, a soothing touch brushed his brow and temples lightly. He felt bolstered and oddly comforted. *Abe!* Noble thought.

Do not give place to fear or doubts, Abe spoke gently into his mind. . . *Your potential greatly outweighs the Enemy, and I also pledge my life to help and protect you!* Noble glanced over at Abe and smiled. Abe's eyes twinkled, but he stared squarely ahead.

Noble noticed that his mother's limp was more noticeable and pronounced. He felt her worry for him, and it pained him that she suffered because of it, because of him. He patted his mother's knee reassuringly as they sat in the pew, he on one side of her and Lark on the other, and waited quietly for the church to fill and for the quiet murmur of voices which spoke in hushed tones to silence.

Pastor Gabriel Hutchins ascended the pulpit and stood, standing sternly, at its podium. This was usually about the time when Noble mentally checked out, for as with many pastors, Pastor Gabriel spoke in a language, an amalgamation of harrumphs, ahems, coughs, and huhhuhs, that did not register or reach the youth of the church, least of all Noble. But Noble endeavored to pay attention, especially since the service was dedicated as a prayer vigil for Piccolo, a close friend of his and especially Lark.

"Greetings, Mt. Sinai," Pastor Hutchins said. "We meet tonight under a frightening and stressful circumstances....."

Just then, the double doors of the sanctuary creaked open, and Nick, dressed in a wrinkled, white, cotton shirt, tie, and old, blue pants that had the hems let out of them, bounded through. He held up one finger in the air, a gesture the older church members used when they wished to be excused from the sanctuary, except that Nick used it to excuse his late entry and made his way through to their pew. Noble felt the eyes of every person on Nick and them. Nick sat next to Genesis first who upon seeing him smiled and patted his back. He then got up and squiggled past her knees and Lark's amid mumbled "'Scuse me's" to plop down unceremoniously next to Noble. Lark leaned forward and stared daggers at him. He smiled sheepishly back at her.

"We meet tonight on a frightening and stressful occasion," Pastor Hutchins repeated. "A trying time, for one of our own is the latest victim in the kidnappings. Who here does not know Piccolo, sweet, shy, and respectful Piccolo, loving daughter of Deacon and Mrs. Thomas? Often we have heard her sing solos in a beautiful voice not unlike the sweet instrument she was named after. We meet tonight not to give in. Not to give up. But to fight. We fight. We pray. And we hope for her safe return....."

His words would have sounded sincere to Noble, if he hadn't noticed Pastor Hutchins admiring his silver and diamond cuff links when he stressed "give in and give up". As he admired his cuff links and the matching ring, Noble noticed a green demon, smaller and less noticeable than the others he had seen, hovering above the Pastor. The demon waggled riches in front of the pastor, chains of gold, amulets, and fine stones from a floating chest of inexhaustible wealth. Of course, no one else noticed it. Noble did not stare at it long for fear of alerting it to his presence. On impulse, Noble turned his attention from the pastor. He surveyed the congregation. Sure enough, a few of the members were shadowed by their own hovering demons. *What did this mean? Was it a total waste of time and energy to be here? If so, what was the point of church? For that matter, what was the point of the fight against the Dark?* Noble searched the congregation still, looking for Mr. Abe. He looked into his eyes questioningly. Mr. Abe smiled again and focused on the pastor. Before long, he heard Mr. Abe's voice in his mind.

"Faith is never a waste of time, Noble," Mr. Abe said. *"Think of the church as a hospital. It is a place where people go to when their souls are sick. As you can see, we live in a sin-sick world, and no one is without his "ills". The Reverend is essentially a good man, Noble. Not perfect but good. And if you look deeper beyond the surface, even beyond the plane where tick-like demons hover as only someone with your power can, you would discover the purity of souls that needs to be protected. These people are good people. You have to believe in them.*

How can I protect them? Noble asked Abe in thoughts.

You have to believe in yourself. You have to simply believe.

Noble couldn't remember when he had stopped believing in church, when the night-time prayers his parents had taught him and the meal blessing had ceased being a potent petition to a higher power and become more of a memorized speech without power or meaning. A litany of phrases and words on the tongue uttered for his mother's approval, forgotten the moment he said Amen and laid his head upon the pillow or he'd swallowed the first bite. Was it sometime after Santa Claus and the Tooth Fairy were proven false? His child-like faith had been so simple then. Is that when he stopped believing? Or was it the moment Noble had learned his father was going away to serve overseas? Pastor Hutchins' words interrupted Noble's thoughts.

"… When the Darkness presses in all around us, we light the candle against the dark to remember that in times like these, we can still dare to believe in goodness, hope, and Light. We light the candle to symbolize the fight that we who love Piccolo pledge to keep our hopes alive until she returns." Pastor Hutchins said. "Miss Lark, will you come sing for your sister?"

Noble glanced at his sister who nodded mutely as she rose to walk towards the pulpit. Pastor Hutchins handed Lark his microphone. Noble knew that with Lark's powerful voice she didn't need it. She accepted the microphone from the pastor politely and closed her eyes as the church pianist began to play.

When Lark sang she retreated to a place where no one could follow her, and Noble's senses told him that she communed with the very essence of air and sound that made music. Her voice was a gift from that place.

> *Why should I feel discouraged*
> *Why should the shadows come*
> *Why should my heart feel lonely*

And long for heaven and home
When Jesus is my portion
A constant friend is he
His eye is on the sparrow
And I know he watches over me
His eye is on the sparrow
And I know he watches me

As she sang the song filled the sanctuary, and her powerful tones reverberated in the ears and bones of all present. The song kept growing, knitting a loving balm around the downtrodden hearts of the Thomases, soothing the troubled and anxious minds of mothers and fathers and all those who feared for the taken children and their own children who had not yet been taken as well. The song kept growing, stretching, climbing, building a wall of protection around the members. The demons who preyed on the soul sick members including Pastor Hutchins fled the building, for they could not bear the sound. Lark held a note that was a clear, clean syllable of pristine air. Lonely, plaintive, the note seemed to call out to another, reaching, and at times pleading for an answer. And as she sang, another voice joined her. A higher blending tone synchronized with Lark's soprano. That voice, which joined Lark's in perfect harmony, was Piccolo's. Lark opened her eyes and sang louder, calling out to it, calling out to her. Piccolo's voice followed. Lark broke her song and called out to Piccolo.

"Piccolo?" she asked. "Pigs is that you? I'm so sorry, Pigs."

"Tell my parents not to worry. I'm not alone. There are others who miss their parents, too."

"Others?" Lark asked. "What others? The other children? Are they okay, too?"

"Yes,... for now," Piccolo answered. "But I don't know for how long. We are all ... asleep. But please tell the Light Bearer to hurry. I don't know how long...."

"Piccolo?" Lark asked. "Pigs!" Larks last call to Piccolo became an anguished scream.

Lark dissolved into inconsolable weeping. Genesis, Abe, and Mr. Bane escorted her from the stage, as she cried heavily into Genesis' shoulder.

The congregation members stared at each other in amazement, and the sanctuary that was filled with the two voices was filled with an excited murmur brought on by the strange occurrences.

Noble patted Lark's back while grabbing his mother and Lark's purses. Genesis wrapped her arms around Lark and led her from the church. Once again, Noble followed behind silently. His shoulders stooped severely under the enormous weight of expectation, doubts, and questions. Nick followed, too.

Mustard Seeds and the Nazarene Tear

"The next part of Training deals with Word Shaping," Mr. Abe said.

This was the eighth training session, and they had learned many remarkable things from Abe and developed their powers: Noble wielded the power of Fire-might, Lark used her voice to render agents of the Dark powerless, and Nick, agile and powerful, honed his fighting skills. At times, Nick's skills rivaled those of Stone, who battled against him to train whenever she came. Unfortunately, Nick practiced only to keep from letting Noble, Lark, and Abe down. He kept his lack of enthusiasm for their training a secret. He didn't have the heart to tell them that he had his own reservations about the Light and faith over all. There were times when he felt like Abe suspected his waning commitment. Abe never said anything to Nick and only smiled at him sad, patient eyes whenever they faced each other. Tenebrous stopped coming altogether. Noble, Nick, and Lark sat in quiet attentiveness in a semi-circle on the floor of Abe's office. Like many times before, Tenebrous and Stone were absent, mysteriously skipping training like they skipped class on occasion at school.

Nick sat between Noble and Lark leaving a mere four inches of personal space between them. Lark fidgeted in irritable discomfort, keenly aware of Nick's stolen glances out of the corner of his eye and the "accidental" brushes and bumps Nick made against her thigh and right forearm. After his fifteenth brush against her leg, Lark rifled through her backpack to find her favorite dictionary, the *Pocket Oxford Dictionary and Thesaurus*. Using both hands, she wacked Nick in the back of his head when Mr. Abe's back was turned.

"Oops," Lark said to Nick. "Forgive me. That was an accident." Noble coughed into his hand to keep from laughing so hard. He also thought he heard Abe's quiet chuckle in his mind, but when Mr. Abe turned to face them, only his eyes twinkled mischievously.

"The Light Worker wields words to shape his reality, especially in battle against the Enemy," Abe continued. "In order for this ability to work, you must exercise strong belief and rid your mind of any doubts, doubt of your mission, doubt of your abilities, even doubt against the Light…"

At Abe's words, Noble wrestled with doubts. They nagged at him and nettled him like the sand gnats that annoyed most of Salvation's residents during the summer and early fall. It was hard enough trying to believe in the impossible task of a fourteen year old doing battle with an ancient, powerful evil force that radiated a malice beyond any boogey man, haunt, or devil he'd had the trouble of taking seriously since childhood, but to believe in an intangible force of goodness when he struggled to overlook conniving conmen, brainwashed, unquestioning sheep-like congregation, and rigid, unbending, cult fanatics who forced you to blindly accept the institutionalized religion that they shamelessly exploited and hid behind, well…. The battle between *the Light and the Darkness* seemed more like a poorly written Manga or comic book and not a quest to save the world at all. Noble worried that he would fail his mother, fail Abe, and all of the innocent souls who so desperately needed him to champion this war. To win the war. Noble sighed. The responsibility of all who needed him wore on him like two tons and his shoulders drooped from their weight.

The individual who considers doubts has the potential to be the strongest believer, Abe spoke into Noble's mind. *You are very perceptive to see the wrong that goes on around you and even the difficulties of the challenges you now face. You are sensitive to all of it, especially since you witness the wrong-doing in a place of enlightenment and love. True, there are people who do not reveal an inherent goodness, who are creatures of motive and manipulation. But consider this: when you look beyond these people, can you not find others, Lighted Ones, who make the community a better place and influence others to do the same? Even the "sick people", those who seek to exploit and confuse, can be made better by the influence of the Lighted Ones. Do not doubt your ability to believe, but rather look at these challenges as opportunities to strengthen your belief.*

Abe then spoke aloud to everyone, "Light Workers wield words to shape their realities, especially in the battle against the Enemy," Abe said. "In order for this ability to be effective, in times of danger, you must picture the image of what you want to appear firmly and clearly in your mind. Luminaries and Light Warriors in the past have used this ability to conjure powerful weaponry, swords, battle axes, scythes, and more to defeat agents of the Enemy. They have manufactured escapes, called needed spiritual artifacts, and saved the lives and souls of many. The stronger your belief, the more powerful the weapon, defensive, or offensive. Belief must be that pure and that strong..." Abe gave Nick another patient, mournful look. Nick glanced away hurriedly, pretending to be more interested in the frayed shoelaces of his worn Adidas sneakers.

"A word of caution..." Abe paused and gave each of them a leveling stare. "The power of belief is nothing to play with. If you shape something into reality using the power of belief and the might of your words and doubt for one moment, your intention will fail or worse backfire against you." Noble noticed that as Abe spoke, his eyes had become hard and frightening, and a fierce storm lurked beneath them as thunder rumbled in the distant sky.

"And if you have the power to believe, then so does your enemy, and being made of pure evil, his capacity for destruction and death is indescribable. Once you have entered into battle with a Dark Minion, you will have no choice but to believe and to fight…to the death…" Noble felt Abe's words weigh heavily on his shoulders and sink further down into his chest; his lungs struggled for air. This was not a game, and for the first time, he considered that he may not survive the quest. Noble and Lark exchanged worried glances. Hearing Noble's thoughts and his sudden panic, Nick opened his eyes in wide alarm for the moment, forgetting to brush his knee against Lark's thigh.

"Until we strengthen your belief, you can practice with these mustard seeds," Abe said. Abe reached into his shirt pocket and pulled out a monogrammed handkerchief. The initials read E. B. A. C. In its folds lay a small hill of golden seeds. They were the same seeds Abe had given him earlier. Abe brought his hand to the faces of Lark, Nick, and Noble. "Place a seed under the tongue and envision what will be in your mind and say it aloud again with the mustard seed firmly underneath your tongue."

Each seed fell from the bowl of Abe's huge, earthen hands. When Noble looked at them again, they appeared like regular seeds, unremarkable. Upon second glance, the seeds glimmered and glowed. Thousands of golden sparkles danced upon the rippling Indian summer air between them, on the ceiling, and on the wall.

"This is a good sign," Abe said. "The seeds of faith recognize your potential as believers."

Lark closed her eyes and pictured a brilliant orange butterfly. "Monarch," she said. The seed evaporated into a million, golden sparkles, settling into a fine, brilliant ochre powder. Moments later, a beautiful, Monarch, six-winged butterfly sprang from the glistening powder, slowing fanning its wings open and closed on Lark's outstretched palm. Lark laughed in amazement and with painstaking gentleness offered her palm to Mr. Abe, Noble, and Nick.

"That's beautiful, Phony," Noble said.

"Yeah," Nick said. "That's cool."

"A messenger being," Abe said. "It carries messages of importance between Lighted Ones. Well done, my young friend."

Nick summoned spinning scimitars with blades that whistled as they cut the air.

"Blades of Wrath," Abe commented. "A formidable weapon against any Dark enemy. It heralds your service as a warrior for the Light, distinctly male and strong." Nick beamed in Abe's praise and twirled them with deft hands and flourish. The shining blades were light in his hands and whistled a deadly song.

"Careful," Abe warned. "Only use them in times of extreme danger. These are not toys and can never be used to harm other innocents or Lightworkers, only minions and agents of the Enemy."

Before the session ended, Lark had conjured a magnificent winged horse the color of a sparkling smoke, and Noble called forth the most spectacular object of all, a dazzling, three-inch, tear-shaped stone, much like a congealed, liquid diamond. Unlike any diamond, the light reflecting from its multi-faceted surface danced and shimmied and bounced and pirouetted in a way that was not typical of how light behaved on this earthly plane. As Noble held it, he felt an intense sadness for the sacrifices made to create it and the hope that the object inspired as it healed thousands throughout time.

"Lightbearer," a soft voice whispered. "Your time is near. You are needed. Hurry to aid the Innocent. Hurry!" The feathery voice echoed and washed over Noble and then faded away altogether.

Noble instinctively knew this was no ordinary "tear". This feat by itself was prodigious, for Noble had not thought about this object or pictured it in his mind. In fact, he had been thinking about how it was possible to safely bring the kidnapped victims home or to find a cure for his mother when the jewel materialized. As he held the glittering object in his hands, he heard a thousand cries and moans and sighs of jubilation and relief. It was a peculiar feeling, and it made him feel lightheaded and dizzy.

Abe's eyes widened in amazement.

"The Nazarene Tear," Abe said. "The Nazarene Tear is capable of stopping the Darkness and binding the curse that keeps the Innocent in captivity. It heals mental, emotional, and physical wounds...."

Noble thought that the diamond was not only capable of curing his mother but also of returning his father to home, so that they could be a real family again. He gazed at it intently.

"... It has been lost for over 100 years, but cannot be summoned, "Abe said.

"Only Elijah, the slave boy who was saved from death, is capable of granting one of pure heart the Tear. Elijah rarely comes to those except in their darkest need. It is nearly an impossible task. But for Elijah to reveal the Tear to you leaves many questions, especially about the depth of your powers and the greatness of your potential, Noble. And more questions about me.... This is very curious, Noble. Very curious, indeed."

Noble clutched the Tear in his hands tightly, and as he did, it began to shimmer and quiver. It floated in the air, revolving in circles and then disappeared.

"We have the Tear, "Noble said. "Why can't we use it now?"

"Because you don't really have the Tear, and you are not ready," Abe said. Noble stared at his empty hands.

"Yes, I am," Noble said, jumping to his feet. Thoughts of rescuing his father and taking away his mother's pain flooded his mind. "You said so yourself. It revealed itself to me!" Noble grabbed the scimitars from Nick's hands mid-swirl, a very risky maneuver made possible by his eagerness, and stuffed them into his school back pack.

"We can stop the Darkness from kidnapping any more children and put an end to this danger that threatens to end our world right now!"

Abe stood up from his winged back chair and regarded Noble with deep sadness and regret. In their sepia depths Noble saw a misery-etched wisdom that had endured many ages. Noble saw the answer within them before Abe spoke it.

"No," Abe said.

"No?" Noble asked. "What do you mean?"

"I mean the Darkness is stronger than you and is far more cunning," Abe said. "I mean that to be a Luminary or Lightworker and face the forces of evil without any help is almost always suicidal, and without the proper training or support.... A fool's task. I know you want to rescue your father and heal your mother. The Darkness knows this, too and will use this against you. I mean you are not ready. Otherwise, it would have remained in your hands."

Noble looked at his feet in anger and desperation. *How many more Innocents would be kidnapped before he was ready? Would he ever be ready enough?*

Yes, you will, Abe answered back. *Patience. Your time is near.*

"With the exception of the scimitars, all elements and elementals that were summoned in your belief must be returned," Abe said to all of them.

"Awwwhhhh," Lark cried out. "Does that mean Midnight has to go, too?" The smoke-colored, winged horse nuzzled Lark's cheek. Tears glistened in her eyes.

"Yes," Abe said smiling gently at Lark. She saw the magical horse and her image reflected in Abe's eyes. "Midnight is not a creature of this realm, and the sustenance he feeds on only exists on his plane. Would you have him to go without?"

"Of course not!" Lark cried. "I love him too much to hurt him."

"Spoken like a true nurturer," Abe said, his eyes twinkling again.

"Will I see him again?" Lark asked, wiping away her tears as she stroked its mane.

"Yes, you will," Abe said. As he spoke the huge butterfly fanned its wings and vanished. Midnight licked Lark's cheek and slowly faded away. "All of the things that you see me do, you will be able to do also."

Noble nodded grimly handing the scimitars back to Nick. He watched quietly as Abe ended the lesson, and hoped against hope that all that Abe said was true. He tried to believe.

10

Mr. M's Lost Faith and an Invitation to Danger

S alvation was a town where some mothers were known to overlook their children. Several wives disregarded the significance of their wedding rings. In turn, quite a few husbands no longer held valid the promises of their vows, but rather viewed them as entanglements. And, as fate would have it, there were fathers who did not father, but forgot the importance of fathering altogether; indeed, those who held such attachments in any kind of regard, held them in name only, providing limited financial support to the offspring they spawned. Such parents dared to buy the most expensive items their hard earned money could buy, but made grossly little investment in moral instruction or mentoring, leaving their sons to figure out the hard lessons of life as best they could, their prodigy often committing the same mistakes they themselves had not learned, stumbling through cycles of generational errors, an endless and uninterrupted legacy.

The well-to-do fared somewhat better, thinking their newly heightened, socio-economic status afforded them a better life free of the perils of poverty and ignorance that they barely escaped themselves. Noble lived in this world: a stark contrast of morals and decency and purpose and high expectations breast fed into him from birth as was his father and his mother and their parents and their ancestors before.

Salvation was a historical town born of the sweat and brawn of slaves and the concrete will of their slave masters, the broken remnant of noble Indian warrior ghosts, and the haunts of greedy Europeans who raped and pillaged and slew and conquered them. Indeed, if one listened closely as he walked among the artfully laid cobblestones on River Main, he could hear the piteous moans and cries of the slaves who laid them. If he looked improperly among the graceful and solemn Live Oaks that lined the beautiful alleys and byways of the village squares, he would spy the swinging corpses of the condemned slaves, for in the times of slavery, judgment was swift, if not just or fair.

Salvation was full of such haunts and spooks, of wandering apparitions of shapeless, floating, phantasms, of unexplained moans and creaks and sighs that could not be explained with the logical mind.

Against and in spite of Salvation's legacy, Noble was brilliant and very keen to perceive the inequities and hypocrisies that existed in the educational system and in life in general. He was not uncaring, but acutely aware of the suffering that went on around him yet at a complete loss for how to respond to it or what to do about it. It was a painful and agonizing existence that showed in an oft-seen furrow that creased his brow and in the concern in his hazel eyes. He did not use slang but spoke crisply and clearly, using an English teacher's diction that he inherited honestly from his English teacher mother, who only allowed standard-English to be spoken in her home. Indeed, his mother spoke seven languages, and he spoke four, but he would not dare let others know that he could. The students that walked the same halls with him at school, took the same classes, and ate the same barely edible school lunch would not be impressed by his abilities.

Noble did not lie, slouch, or slack. His pants did not sag. He wore no flashy gold jewelry or boasted any designer brands. He displayed no mysterious tattoos, but he found that having an erect posture was but one more of the million and one things that set him at odds with his peers. He was brutally and tactlessly honest, often at the painful retaliation of teens and adults alike.

But more than anything, he had an uncanny ability to discern when something was not quite right. It was a peculiar and heady sensation of rot and sulfur, spoil and unnamed, unearthly fumes. The shifty eye. The twitchy finger. A mouth that boasted too many words but revealed nothing. All of things revealed glimpses of glaring truths that he often did not want to see. These were the gifts of the Luminary to be able to see through the Veil of the spirit realms, Abe told him. Noble felt more cursed by the abilities than gifted.

Just today in history class, he was half-listening to the monotone dribble of his uncaring teacher, Mr. Don Malacadem, who as usual, offered half-truths, spewed erroneous information, and broadcasted outdated lore about the history of chess. Noble was just thinking in the peculiar way he did of paying attention to all things at once -- the tic-tic-tic of the clock on the wall, the underhanded way that Drew Hanson picked his nose and ate the contents of such under a covered hand, the rise and fall of a full breast of a teen girl with angry eyes-- while being keenly aware of his own thoughts, of why the history of chess was so important in an *American* History class? It wasn't as if the game originated in America. Like all great inventions, literature, and ideals of noble pursuit, the game was stolen, imported, or borrowed from other cultures and civilizations.

"...The game of chess originated in Spain. The queen piece being named for Queen Isabella..." Mr. Malacadem said.

Noble sighed and rolled his eyes heavenward. Dr. Malacadem was six years, eight months and ten days from retirement, and he did not expend one bit of energy that hindered him from attaining that goal. On his wall today hung the same faded, gum-studded poster that hung on the wall 15 years ago: *Climb Every Mountain*, it read. The import of the words was lost to the unconcerned students of unknown aims and even fewer goals that filled his classroom day after day in PS 119. Half of the students slept, gossiped, or daydreamed their way through school. The only student who cared was Noble, and as usual, he wrestled an impulse to correct his insensible and ineffective teacher -- again.

Against all that was cool and socially acceptable, against his already sub-status on the social hierarchy of peers, against all that was logical, Noble raised his hand. Dr. Malacadem droned on for another four minutes before he even noticed Noble's upraised hand. In fact, he had just noted when the Chen twins interrupted their long going conversation on just who Miles Townsend was dating this fall. He followed their stares, along with everyone else's to Noble. Another fifteen seconds, an eternity, passed.

"Mmmm, yes?" Dr. Malacadem asked.

"You're wrong," Noble mumbled.

"Come again?" Dr. Malacadem asked.

"You are wrong in your assertion," Noble said. He then added, "*Sir*".

Dr. Malacadem took off his glasses and rubbed them once again with a handkerchief, a gesture of practiced patience more so of cleanliness. He took a deep breath and visibly counted to ten.

"Class, once again, *Dr.* Goodson chooses to instruct us against the text's authors, researchers, and experts." Dr. Malacadem cleared his throat, a gesture made more in contempt than with a cough. Noble thought that Mr. Malacadem's eyes glowed yellow with black slits for pupils, but as Noble stared at him more intently, he noticed they were his regular, dark brown with his trademark scowl. And his eyes held more malice and cruelty than Noble ever knew Dr. Malacadem to show.

"Do tell," he said. Noble braced himself for the onslaught of Dr. Malacadem's attack. *Newsflash: Retard-lunatic gives lecture to a class of morons. When would he ever learn?*

"Chess," Noble said, "or El Chautrang originated in India. The conquering Moors traveled to India and carried the game back to Africa, where they developed a version of the game to create and practice war strategy. As the Moors invaded Italy, Portugal, and Spain, they influenced the cultures they invaded with their own customs. Spain developed a version of the game that included a queen piece, named for Queen Isabella, a convention that would never have been practiced in Northern Africa, for the Moors' women were not allowed the power to fight or to rule..."

"Is it over yet?" asked one student. Her nose, forehead, and upper lip were pierced with silver studs. She was completely bald save for an auburn Mohawk that crowned her ebony head. She blew a bubble the size of a grapefruit, popped it with a reverberating bang, and pulled the pink mass back inside her mouth again for further attack. The clamor sounded like rapid gun fire. Some students hit the floor in jest. Others laughed at the interruption her stunt had caused. She turned around to face Noble and made a crude gesture with her tongue and fingers, revealing a tongue pierced with a silver skull whose mouth was frozen in a silent scream. Noble raised his eyebrows. She smiled at his reaction and winked.

How many piercings could the human body possibly take? Noble wondered.

The Chen sisters continued their conversation on who dated who, who cheated, and who was on the rebound. It was no secret that this was their third time taking AP U.S. History. That Noble was an underclassman, a freshman, the youngest person known to take an AP upper level history class did not endear him to his classmates. And now once again, he dared to interrupt the boring monotone monologue that was Mr. Malacadem's meaningless blah-blah-blah.

Noble tried not to look around him. Since his powers were growing, he saw more and more of the misery and abuse and disappointment and pain and fear and sorrow than he wanted to see in humanity caused by the soul's vulnerability to spirits and demons and evil influences. Evil was everywhere! And he didn't want to see that either. Since his recent initiation into the Light-workers and Luminaries, he missed his mundane existence even more. He just wanted to be normal.

Half of the class slept during Noble's explanation, drooling or snoring, never mind Mr. Malcadem's lecture. One freckle-faced boy with ginger dreads suffered from sleep apnea. His ragged snores punctuated the lapses of painstaking breathlessness. Two football players, dressed in the blue and orange jerseys of their team's colors, stuck feathers, strings, and toothpicks down the sleeping boy's open mouth and nostrils. They placed bets on how far they could place a dice cube tied to a string down his throat before he would wake up.

Mr. Malacadem was just placing the stamps on the envelopes of bills he'd written out when a knock at the door interrupted. He shoved his checkbook and bills into his desk drawer and grabbed his pointer, making a show to point to notes on the Sumerians that had been on the board weeks ago. Melody Stevens, a petite and pretty girl the color of a banana fig, entered the room and stood in front of Mr. Malacadem.

"Excuse me, Mr. M," Melody said. Her shoulder length braids were gathered into a side pony tail that cascaded over her left shoulder. Just last week, Melody winked at Noble behind the long, flirty bangs of an otherwise ultra-short haircut. She personalized her white polo uniform shirt and pleated, navy uniform skirt with a pink argyle sweater, pink argyle socks, and matching pink, argyle ribbons that adorned her pony tail. She waived to several of her friends and smiled at even more admiring boys who recognized her celebrity status on campus.

"May I make an announcement to your class, Sir?" she asked Mr. Malacadem.

"Of course, Dear,`" Mr. Malcadem said. His eyes leered at Melody's form. Noble didn't like the way Dr. M followed her every move with his eyes, like a predator stalking its prey. It reminded him of the way his godfather Cypress looked at his mother. Noble sensed evil all around Dr. Malacadem. Having placed his pointer back in its habitual, dusty spot on the desk, he continued to lick stamps and place them on the envelopes of his car note and bills. Noble wanted to yell at him that stamps were self-adhesive and that they didn't need to be licked anymore, but Melody held his attention more.

"The student council and the class of 2012 would like to invite you to the homecoming dance Friday night at 8:00 p.m. in the school auditorium," Melody said. Her ribbons flitted prettily as she read from her memo. "Admission is five dollars and a canned good to be donated to the community food pantry for Thanksgiving. I hope to see you there." She toyed with the ribbon tied braid over her shoulder. Several of the boys and the even the tattooed, pierced girl were mesmerized by the gesture.

And then she smiled, revealing the most perfect dimples and even, white teeth Noble had ever seen. Noble's stomach somersaulted ...

Dance Friday night? Noble's thoughts of Melody were abruptly interrupted. With all of the recent kidnappings, Noble considered that an evening dance filled with dozens of teens was probably the most unsafe place for the students at PS 119.

"But what about the kidnappings?" Noble asked.

"The dance, Mr. Goodson," interrupted to Mr. Malacadem, "Would be a good opportunity for the students to take their minds off the recent events. It's just what we *all* need."

"Don't you think that it would be safer for the students to stay at home?" Noble asked.

"No, *Dr.* Goodson," Mr. Malacadem said. "I do not think it would be unsafe, only boring if *you* were there." Mr. Malacadem smiled triumphantly as the class jeered and cheered at his comment.

"Yeah," one student said, interrupting the pages of doodles he scribbled in his notebook.

"Whatever you do, please don't show up," another student said.

"Stay home!" the girl with the multiple piercings yelled. She'd already begun to text all of her friends about the upcoming party Friday night.

"There aren't any lectures at dances!" said Mr. Malacadem. "You have no friends. You're weird. You mumble to yourself. You spout unnecessary information that no one cares about. What is it that you students say these days? Yes, you're a loser!" Making an L with his right pointer finger and thumb, he placed the gesture against his receding hairline. The children laughed. Noble looked at Mr. Malacadem, clutching the sides of his desk. He tried to quell the angry storm that roared inside of him. His cheeks burned and his ears turned crimson in anger and embarrassment. He glanced over at Melody, who cast a look of concern, sadness, and a funny expression that Noble surmised was pity.

After hearing Mr. Malacadem's insult, he ripped one side of his school desk away from the chair. Noble thought fleetingly of Abe's reminder to not reveal his strengths and powers in public and to refrain from acting in anger. But Noble's anger at Mr. Malacadem and his embarrassment held his attention more. Holding the metal and wooden side in his hand made him look crazy which only made him more furious.

"Look everyone," Mr. Malacadem said. "I believe we've made someone upset. Did we hurt your feelings?"

The class was a circus of deriding laughter, jests, and insults. The students scorned him. His teacher taunted him. And the one girl he admired in the entire school felt ashamed for him. It was more than he could bear.

As he looked around the room at the jeering faces, he caught a whiff of sulfur and fumes. He noticed that each person wore a frozen laugh or glare. The second hand on the clock stuck. The fly on the window sill remained motionless, and even the Chen sisters were frozen in a conspiring, frozen huddle over the girl with piercings. Noble looked up and noticed a floating entity, its body resembling a human man. The ghoulish phantasm was transparent and gray, and its robes were murky smoke. Red eyed and toothsome, it grinned wickedly at Noble, winked and waved. It dumped an urn of what looked like ashes and refuse over Noble's head: crumbling bones, fragments of bony fingers, broken watch pieces, torn dolls. Noble noticed that the more refuse the demon dumped over him, the heavier and hotter and angrier he felt. Noble had always seen demons attacking others; he'd never been the victim of one himself.

Noble looked around for Mr. Abe wondering if he had stopped time.

"No use wasting your time looking for your friend the custodial worker," Mr. Malacadem said. His red eyes had turned the blackest of black, and their centers held not pupils, only evil, crimson slits. "Your savior isn't here. This is a shade," Mr. Malacadem indicated waving his now full set of talons at the floating entity. They don't do much for souls, but they can do a lot of damage to the likes of us, especially you, Son of Light."

Mr. Malacadem ran his six inch talons along the delicate skin of Melody's neck. Immediately, the delicate skin beneath his touch began to well and pucker. She whimpered in pain as it turned red and then bruised purple. Her face was still a beautiful mask of pity and concern. Mr. Malcadem smiled at her discomfort. Noble realized that he could kill her, would kill her and nothing would be left of the person that visited his dreams and haunted his fantasies but a pile of dust. He could do it. Noble waited, not daring to move, not even daring to breathe. Noble searched his mind for every lesson Mr. Abe had taught him, frantic for a way to save Melody. He had to get rid of the shade first. Noble realized that Mr. Malacadem was quite a good chess player after all: he had Noble considering his next move that would result in the fewest casualties as possible.

"Ashes and dust," Noble whispered, and as he spoke the being disintegrated into a cloud of ash. It rained ashes as if a flurry of snow drifted in the room. Like a Chesire cat, only its glowing eyes and wicked smile remained. They at last faded, too. Noble noticed that he didn't feel as angry or ashamed as he had before and his thoughts were clearer, sharper. He focused again on Mr. Malcadem and Melody, hoping that they would understand the danger they were in.

"Melody," Noble said. "Please. Don't go. It's not safe. It's not safe for any of us!" Noble turned toward the class, staring imploringly. Noble knew she could not move, but he felt with all his heart that she could hear him.

"I have to go," Melody said in a sad, sing-song voice. "I'm commanded to go. Mr. Malacadem snapped his talon-tipped fingers, allowing her to move. Her eyes were dull and vacant. "I'm on the student council." With much effort, she cast him her own pleading look and exited the room quietly, absently rubbing the burning welt on her throat. Her body and face moved with a will that wasn't her own, a zombie, her braided ponytail bouncing behind her against her shoulder and back.

"Mr. Malacadem, what happened to you?" Noble asked. Noble stared back at Mr. Malacadem again, wondering what had happened to him to make him so bitter, so cynical, and so uncaring.

"You mean you don't know," Mr. Malacadem asked. Mr. Malacadem placed the tip of the talon laced with Melody's blood to his lips and tasted its sweetness. He quivered in ecstasy.

Just as he did, the air above Mr. Malacadem rustled and roiled, as if waves of steam were rippling above a steaming kettle. A confident man, a happy man full of energy and hope, years younger without the receding hair line and bald spot he had today, sat at a table in a humble kitchen. He held a letter in his hands. With shaking excitement, he handed it to an elderly woman with carefully waved, silver hair. She searched in her apron and pulled a pair of reading glasses from her pocket. She placed them on her face.

"You've been accepted to Julliard." She read. Mr. Malacadem waited.

"Yes, Momma!" the young man said beaming when she didn't answer. His eyes and face were alight with eagerness and hope. "I've been accepted into their program for the arts. My concentration is in dancing. Momma, do you know what this means? I can dance! I can dance, Momma! I told you I could do it!"

The elderly woman folded the paper into neat thirds and handed it back to her son.

"Momma, did you hear me? I can go away to study dance and become a professional dancer. Maybe I can become a choreographer. A professor. Maybe even a performer for the Alvin Ailey Dance Company! Isn't it wonderful?"

"How will you pay for this school?" the elderly woman asked, wiping off the kitchen counter. She rinsed a pile of potatoes in her sink and began to peel them. Her wrinkled, eggplant hands worked quickly as she whisked the peeler across the surface of one potato and then another. Each peeled potato plopped into a pot of water.

"There's a partial scholarship!" the young man said. He unfolded the letter and turned to the second page, pointing to the scholarship.

"Hmmm," the elderly woman said, continuing to peel. *Plop!* went another potato into the pot of water.

"I'll get a job. Two jobs to pay for the rest, the tuition, a place to stay while I study."

"That's not practical, Son. Going all the way to New York to take up a trade that won't put food on your table or a roof over your head. And what about your sister and her education? Will dancing pay for that, too?"

"Then I'll work three jobs until I join a company. *And I'll pay* for her education."

"Teaching. Now there's a fine, solid job! It's a sensible job for a man, a real man, and not some fairy skipping and sashaying around the stage!" She placed the folded envelop onto the counter before returning to her work. *Plop! Plop! Plop!* More potatoes dropped into the pot.

The young man stood up from the table, clenching the letter into a tight fist. He picked up the community college envelope from the table and grabbed the applications his mother saved for him for teaching school. His shoulders drooped and his head hung low. He looked like a man who had lost his very soul. Without a word, he tossed the letter from Julliard into the kitchen trash can and left the kitchen with the catalog and application forms in his arms.

The memory flickered, roiled, flickered again and vanished. This time the image revealed a slightly older Mr. M in a hurtling split that placed his rushing legs parallel with the bar. He twirled and fell, cracking his ankle. Tears welled in his eyes, for at that moment he realized that he could barely keep up his studies at both school and hold down his two jobs. As his dream slipped away, ... Noble examined the *Climb Every*

Mountain poster that hung on the wall above Mr. Malacadem's desk. Beneath the faded words was a picture of dancer, his arms spread in a wide, dramatic arc and his back arched gracefully. It was the young man in the memory. It was Mr. Malacadem.

Noble looked again at Mr. Malacadem and looked deep within his eyes.

"If you don't stop this dance, another student or many students will not get the opportunity to live out their dreams," Noble said.

Mr. Malacadem jumped up, staring at Noble with alarm. He sprang back from the chair as if he had been stung by a scorpion, and he fixed Noble with an icy stare.

"What would you know about crushed dreams or disappointment?" he asked. "What if the whole world, your mother who never believed in you, your sister who needed someone to look after her, all depended on you? What if you had to put your dreams on hold, bury them, for the sake of responsibility and duty? Do you have any answers for that *Dr. Goodson?*" Mr. Malacadem yelled and his voice melted into sobs. Noble listened in silence. Somehow he knew that Mr. Malacadem's words were private and hurtful to share. In the midst of sobbing, Mr. Malacadem's lips formed into a slow, malicious smile. He then opened his mouth to laugh in dry, voiceless laugh.

"Yeah," I hope they do go to the dance tonight, and I hope the Darkness snatches more souls," Mr. Malacadem said.

Noble eyes widened and his heartbeat skipped.

"Yes, I serve the Darkness, Son of Light," Mr. Malacadem said. As he spoke, his sepia skin turned an ashen grey, and the whites of his eyes turned green, then a glowing, sulfur yellow. His mouth enlarged to accommodate rows of teeth that were impossible for a human face and horns grew from the bald pate of his head. "Hello, Son of Light. I've taken this dopey school teacher. He doesn't even know that he's being used. Tonight, I look for sacrifices to fulfill my destiny, The Blood of Seven,

THROUGH A GLASS DARKLY

The Innocent, the not so innocent. Teens and children alike will pay a cruel price."

The demon inside of Mr. Malacadem leered at Noble and then laughed a wicked grin. A miniature windstorm swept through the class room, ripping the posters off the walls, and the papers off the desks. It exited the room in a swoosh, leaving Mr. Malaadem fatigued and suddenly alert as if he were waking from a dream.

"Where was I?" Mr. Malcadem asked. He looked wide-eyed, physically nettled, and taken unawares. "Did that Stevens girl make her announcement already? Yes, the dance. Right. All those interested should consult their homeroom teachers during advisement period today. Now back to our lecture on chess. Queen Isabella is named for the queen's piece...."

As Mr. Malacadem finished his lecture, Noble cast his mind at Nick and Lark. *Where are you two?* he asked.

He needed to talk to the principal to prevent the dangerous function in school. Noble hoped that the principal would prevent the unnecessary abductions and possible sacrifices from happening. Well before the bell rang, Noble rushed out of class to warn him.

On his way down the hall, he tried Lark again. Nick could not get away from running laps around the gym for teasing one of the athletes who constantly tormented the new freshmen who dropped the ball.

Lark.... Phony, where are you?

He cast out his mind in all directions as Abe had shown him. He located her life force in study hall.

... His lips crushed hers in an overpowering kiss. His hungry tongue darted out and parted her waiting lips....

Really Phony! Can't you find a better use of your time, or at least better reading material!

"Nobby!" she growled. She stood up stiff and indignant. "There is such a thing as privacy!" She looked around her noticing the students' curious glances and blushed.

"Sorry," she offered to them. "A really good book!" She shifted to speaking in her mind.

Go ahead to the principal's office. I'll meet you there.

Noble knocked on the principal's door and found it locked. The secretary informed him that he had left school early to attend a Board meeting downtown. He looked around for the assistant principal's office door. Without knocking, he rushed in. He found his god father, Cypress Bane, sitting at his desk lost in thought. He nursed a cold cup of tea.

Noble approached.

"Mr. Bane?" Noble asked.

Mr. Bane raised his eyebrows quizzically.

"You have to stop this party this evening," Noble asked.

"On what grounds?" Cypress asked.

"On the certainty that there will be another kidnapping, possibly a killing," Noble answered.

"Certainty?" Cypress asked lacing his fingers together across his desk. "What certainty?"

"Surely you must know of the danger---" Noble said. And then in a lower voice, "As a member of the Light."

"What nonsense is this?" Cypress asked, springing up from behind his desk. As usual, he wore an impeccable, dark suit and tie. He put his hand on Noble's shoulders and looked meaningfully in Noble's eyes. "Surely silly talk of Light groups will land you in detention..... *If not dead...*"

Noble knew his god-father was in the Community of Light, but other than his presence at his Trial, he had never seen or heard him use his own powers. He listened intently as he spoke in his mind.

You would be wise to refrain from speaking of our Brotherhood in public, Noble. It only draws attention from the Enemy. I thought your smiling mentor would have taught you better. You place all of us in peril with such recklessness.

Noble stared into Cypress's eyes with anger. What did his life matter when so many would be hurt and possibly the world ended? He held back his feelings and his words and listened, resisting the urge to yell out at Cypress.

"What about the party tonight, Sir," Noble asked. "It's not safe."

"I'm afraid that if you have no proof to offer of any real danger, the party will proceed as planned," Cypress said.

Noble shook off Cypress's hand from his shoulder and stared at him blankly, not believing that his god-father would not assist in stopping the killings.

"Is there anything more I can do for you, Son?" Cypress asked. By Cypress's tone, Noble could tell that the conversation had concluded. Without waiting for Noble to answer, he resumed his seat at his desk and returned to his cool tea. "Give your regards to your mother."

"That is the last thing I will do," Noble said slamming his god-father's door.

11

A Change in Venue

Mourner's Row Park was created at the edge of Whispering Woods during the late sixties by the city's recreational department. The park was developed to put a friendlier face on a disturbing area of Salvation's beautiful landscape with an even more unsettling past. Most grandparents who lived today were young enough to hear their own parents' talk of the menacing wilds that many slaves braved to escape brutal slave owners. And even then, the desperate slave fled reluctantly, weary of the looming, fearful, Live Oaks with limbs that seemed to snatch and grapple at passersby or the inhuman cries of terror that silenced all the natural noises of the woods: no happy, chirpy larks or robins or fluttering blue jays; no humming bees or buzzing insects; not even the cheerful croak of a lonesome frog. Nothing. Nothing but the sinister gales hissing through the trees:

> *Nothing of the Light dwellsssssss ... here....*
> *Ssssolemn sssoundsssss of weeping and gnashing*
> *of Dark seizing, snatching*
> *No Good Livesss Here*

And when the wind did not whisper, some people said that not even the runaway slaves were able to outrun whatever lurked in those woods. *So what poor creatures moaned and cried in open night air? Since when had the night associated with the murderous allies of the dark?*

Sssssssssssssssssssssss ... No Good Livesss Here!!!!!

It was no wonder that no one in all the history of Salvation remembered a slave escaping the horror of the woods, not one. And as an evil reminder, one of the last sights that barred the desperate runaway from escaping through the Whispering Woods was a gruesome memorial of Slavery's savage brutality: Twelve gruesome trees that served as hanging posts stood silently against the howling wilderness where many a slave was burned, castrated, butchered, and then finally hung. What had made Nick choose such a grisly location for the school party, Nick did not know, but he was strangely silent. It was like some deadly purpose had reached out to him, called him, and compelled him to move the party to this location, and he was powerless to refuse it. That was the frightening part.

Be careful to guard your minds, Abe taught them. *The war against the Dark is as much of an internal struggle of thoughts and emotions as it as an external one of flesh and steel. We must be trained to fight demons and we must fight the demons that plague our minds, too ... And above all, never let down your guard. The Dark attacks when you least expect it. Be vigilant!*

Nick summoned the water basin imagery as Abe had taught them during training, but as with many things he and Noble did together, Nick did not take the training seriously. He counted on Noble to be his walking cheat sheet should the need arise. And now, Noble wasn't there.

They had agreed to meet before the first students arrived. Nick had gone ahead to scout the area and begin organizing the set for the "secret" party. It was funny how they'd come up with the idea to have a "secret" party. Everyone knew that most kids did the opposite of what they were told. Moreover, if they had to choose between a party that was chaperoned by adults and one where no one was going to tell them that they were dancing too close or what music to listen to or if the music was too loud or what time to go home, there was no guessing as to which party they would choose.

The "secret" party ended up being no secret at all. Nick knew to tell Kiara who most people knew could not keep a secret. Half of the school knew about the event 30 minutes after he told her. By sixth period, the entire student body was buzzing about the "secret" party. The only people who were not clued in were the adults, and that was the most fun of all. The kids got a big kick out of knowing that the adults would expect them to be at the dance since it was the first social event of the school year. The trick was making the kids follow the rules without being told to do so. Nick proved resourceful on this matter, too. He planned to have too few refreshments so that they would run out well before the party was in full swing. It was always cooler and darker at Mourner's Row so without enough lighting, most kids would be inclined to leave early. Nick thought of everything. Many times Noble wondered how Nick could get such low grades when he was really a pure genius.

"Honestly, why do you even bother to come to school?" Noble had asked Nick so many times before when he usually said or did something that showed his keen intelligence. "You could be an honor graduate or finish school early. Why do you do so poorly?"

"I'm just biding my time until I can start my career in comedy," Nick said with a wide grin. "Besides, school's just an institution of the establishment." And like so many times before, Noble would roll his eyes or shake his head.

Tables were already set up in the middle of the grassy area, and DJ Raw Beats, really Joey Evans, a technology geek sophomore who gained popularity last year when he played for the homecoming dance, began setting up the speakers for the music. Soon the boom-boom-boom was deafening as students began to trickle in. A table cloth was spread halfway across one of the tables, as if something had hastily interrupted their work or they had been called away. Nick made to finish the tables when without warning, the moaning and whispering voices beckoned. Nick's feet seemed to move with a will of their own beyond the clearing, beyond the hanging posts, and into the dark, dark shadows and the bare, looming tree limbs. The shadows reached out to him and swallowed him.

Noble made it to Mourner's Park minutes before the first kids arrived. For once, he felt excited and relieved that maybe, just maybe, he could beat this thing, The Darkness, and that maybe, just maybe, the children would be safe and free. At least he could prevent more kidnappings from occurring. And then he heard an evil chuckle in his mind. The music blared from the loud speakers. Raw Beats worked the crowds, scratching the records between two turn tables. The teens milled onto the open field, gyrating and leaping, bouncing and jolting. Noble looked down at his clothes and began to feel a little self-conscious. Most of the kids wore tee shirts and jeans and sneakers. While he wore his own jeans, he felt a little out of place in his freshly pressed shirt. Lark had burst into his room at the last minute, insisting on the orange plaid.

"Wear this," Lark said, shoving the shirt beneath his nose. "It compliments your skin and brings out the color in your eyes."

Not wanting to argue and pressed for time, Noble relented. He gazed across the field at Lark, who wore her own pair of jeans, a white peasant blouse, and sandals. A white ribbon adorned her curls. Two boys flocked around her as she toyed with a drink in her hand. Noble fought the compulsion to hurl fire orbs at the boys. She immediately looked up and stared at Noble.

I'm okay, Nobby. I can handle myself, she spoke into his mind.

We are supposed to be working! he said, projecting his thoughts into her mind.

I am! She fired back. *"It just so happens that I'm able to look out for the Darkness and have a little fun at the same time.*

Every so often she glanced around the fields to survey the kids. Both Nick and Lark had agreed to patrol the action on the field at the party

95

while Noble walked among the crowds to make sure everyone was safe. Noble glanced around the field.

Where's Nick? he asked, projecting his question into Lark's mind.

Don't know. I thought he was with you, Lark answered back. Noble could feel her worry.

Noble shook his head no. He hadn't seen Nick since they had cooked up this crazy scheme to shift locations of the party to prevent another kidnapping at a well-publicized event. That was hours ago. He had also been trying to reach Abe for hours, but for some reason he couldn't reach his mind. He knew Abe was more than capable of taking care of himself, but he could not help worrying about him, too.

Noble wound his way through the throng of rotating and bounding bodies.

"Why is it that the only dances kids know involve pelvic thrusts and shaking butts?" he asked aloud to no one in particular.

"I rather like shaking my derriere," Melody Stevens said. She stood right beside him in the crowd of dancing teens, smiling wickedly. Noble swallowed nervously. She wore an orange sundress that revealed her ebony back and shoulders. Her braids were spiraled into curls that cascaded down her back.

"Melody---," Noble said. "I didn't see you."

"I didn't think you did," she said smiling again. "Do you often hold conversations with yourself?"

Ten seconds had passed before Noble realized he was standing there with his mouth open. He shut it and thought of something to say before he made himself look even dorkier than he was.

"Not too often," he said. He stared at her, not believing she had actually singled him out in conversation. There were dozens of guys who vied for her attention, and here she was standing here, talking to him.

"You're strange, Noble, but different," Melody said, her dimples creasing her lovely, chocolate cheeks. "That's why I like you. You're not like everybody else." She stood there waiting for him to respond, playing with the ends of a curl. "Well, aren't you going to ask me?"

"Ask you what?" Noble asked.

"To dance, of course," she said, her brown eyes teasing.

"Dance?" Noble asked. He stared down at his white sneakers and thought, *It's now or never. I probably won't get this opportunity again.* "Would you like to dance?"

"I thought you'd never ask," she said.

Nick stumbled into the dark woods. He cast frantic glances all around him. In every direction, the dark crowded in around him, offering him no means of escape. How had he gotten here into Whispering Woods? Nick looked up. The black trees blocked a starless sky. The winds whispered and howled at him, mocking his helplessness. He shivered. His jeans were ripped and torn along his pant legs as if he traveled far across the underbrush deep into the sinister copse. Even his legs stung as if they were scratched in his unremembered journey into the cursed stretch of wilderness.

Nick strained in the deep blackness to hear the sounds of the party, the music, or even the celebrating kids. He heard nothing. Nothing but the howling and the whispering. He could not shake the feeling that something evil and malignant watched him and waited.

Nick stumbled on. He halted suddenly, straining to listen. His heart thudded in his ears. He heard it. Crying and whimpering. Nick hastened to the sound, daring not to speak. A clearing broke in the trees overhead, permitting a weak moonbeam from the pale moon overhead to illuminate a ghostly figure. As he crept closer he saw her. A lone girl with waist length hair and full breasts wept into her hands. Her skirt was ripped, revealing shapely thighs and calves. Scratches covered her bare arms and her shoulders shook with her weeping.

As Nick crept closer still, a dry twig snapped beneath his ripped sneakers, betraying his presence. She jumped back, holding her arms up in a protective gesture. Even her tear-stained face was beautiful. Large, deep brown eyes stared back at him, startled. She wiped at the tears on her soft cheeks with the back of her hand and bit her full lips.

"What—What do you want?" she asked.

"Are you okay?" Nick asked stepping closer. "I won't hurt you."

She stared back at him with fear and distrust in her large, brown eyes.

"Are you lost?" Nick asked. He exhaled in relief. "I'm lost, too. Maybe we can find our way out of this place together."

The girl nodded, sniffing, and crept closer. Nick took off his navy sweater and slowly offered it to her. She accepted the sweater cautiously and wrapped it around her scratched arms and shoulders. She smiled.

"My name's Nick," Nick said. "What's yours?"

She merely nodded.

"You don't have to tell me your name," Nick said. "Silence is good. I'm just glad for your company."

To this the girl stood up revealing full breasts beneath a thin, cotton sheath. She threw her arms around Nick and buried her head in his chest. Nick patted her back awkwardly.

"I'm not much of the hugging kind," Nick said. The girl cried harder. "But hugging's good, too. I guess. Listen. We have to find our way out of here. How did you get here? Did you wake up here, too?"

Her grip tightened around Nick, and he wriggled in her embrace.

"You're kinda' strong, aren't you?" Nick asked. "Not that this isn't flattering, but do you mind loosening your grip on me so I can breathe?"

The girl's shoulders shook as if she were crying into his chest. Nick patted her back again clumsily.

"There's no need to be upset," Nick said. "We'll get out of this. You'll see."

The girl's shoulders shook harder, but as Nick patted her back he tensed in her embrace. The first frissons of alarm snaked up his back and behind his neck. His hair stood up on end in those places. Something did not feel right. Something was wrong, and he felt danger.

"That's just it," an evil voice answered. "You won't get out of this, at least not in one piece." Nick froze. The deep, beastly voice sounded as if it came from all around him, but a sinking feeling in his stomach and chest told him that it was the girl who had spoken. Frightened, he broke away from the girl's tight embrace and stumbled back. The girl stumbled back, too, but not so much from Nick as from what Nick discovered was her laughing.

"Are you going to protect, po' little ol' helpless me?" she asked. Her voice was deep and terrifying. As she spoke her skin turned green, and her face and body lost some of its voluptuousness and curves. Her body lengthened, and her eyes glowed a smoldering red. Black talons grew from the ends of her bony, green fingers.

"You ain't so helpless, are you?" Nick said. Shaking, he backed away from her slowly like one would back away from a cotton mouth poised for strike.

"Don't you want to give me a kiss?" the demon asked. Her black talons grew to over three inches, and fangs appeared at the corners of her wicked smile.

"I'll pass," Nick said. "I usually go for the more demure type. Less fangs and creepiness. More cute and cuddly."

"You are quite funny," the demon girl said. "What a shame to waste such humor and talent."

"Exactly," Nick said backing farther away. "So why don't we part ways peacefully? I'll go my way and you can get back to being ---creepy or whatever."

Nick turned slowly, baring his scimitars, their shiny blades whistled in the wind. He backed away, his eyes searching for avenues of escape. He found a narrow clearing through the trees and ran. He made it a few steps before the demon reappeared in front of him, blocking his exit. She sprang on top of him, knocking him to the forest floor. With an inhuman strength, she penned him to the ground, burying his face in the dirt. The demon's voice turned masculine, and with strong, monstrous, man-like arms, she tore his belt from his waist and ripped his jeans down his thighs and away from his body. Nick felt the demon's hot breath on his neck and a roughness on her cheek that felt like the harshness of beard stubble. Nick opened his mouth to scream *No!* and more hands covered his mouth and held his face down in the dirt and abrasive underbrush. It scratched his face and neck. The monster, no longer the deceptive, crying girl but a beast, entered him roughly from behind. He tasted dirt and fear and bile ---- pain. *NO!-NO!-NO!-NO!-nononononononon onooooooooooooooooooo!* The world he remembered, the world he knew died in that moment of viciousness and pain and violation, and everything around him went black.

Noble offered his arm and Melody took it. As he led her further into the crowd, Raw Beats played a slower, love song. Noble faced Melody and placed his palms awkwardly around her waist. She laced her fingers behind his neck, and they swayed slowly in time to the music. She leaned into him, laying her head upon his chest. He inhaled slowly, smelling the gardenia scent of her sweet perfume. For a moment, he closed his eyes, forgetting about the Innocent, forgetting about the battle between Light and Dark, forgetting about Light Warriors and demons, forgetting about being the Light's Champion, and he just let himself live in this moment.

It was a sweet moment, born of all the dreams he dreamt of her and of all the times he had imagined holding her. Only better. Lightning bugs sparkled in the twilight over the dancing students. Frogs croaked happily. *Had he conjured them?* He closed his eyes and imagined that they were alone and the music played only for them. Her arm brushed against his cheek. It was smooth and warm, softly scented with her sweet perfume. He breathed her in. In his mind, he imagined her raising her head to kiss him. Her lips moved closer, her cheek nuzzling against his. He could smell her sweet, warm breath.

Noble opened his eyes. It wasn't a dream. Melody's eyes were closed and her lips hovered inches from his. Her lips were soft and trembling.

They gently brushed against his before parting, and he tasted the sweet taste of her mouth. He would remember this dance, this kiss, this moment for the rest of his life.

Noble glanced around the gathering of gyrating teens. He felt a familiar sensation of foreboding: a sinking in the pit of his stomach, a tingling in the back of his neck and forearms, and the hair in these areas standing on end.

The magic of the kiss was broken. A force that was more than an inkling compelled him to look at his sister. A quick glance revealed the same two male admirers who hovered around Lark earlier. Their body language revealed mild flirting: Lark laughed coquettishly over her plastic cup. Blythe Bohman, a popular senior who held the reputation of a player, leaned forward from his casual lean against the loud speaker to share a joke. They both shared a laugh.

Blythe competed for Lark's attention with another beau, a tall, wiry teen Noble had never seen before. He had straight, black, shoulder-length hair and wore a floor length, black, leather coat, smoke leather pants, and boots. But the peculiar quality that made Noble feel uncomfortable was the pair of sunglasses the stranger wore that hid his eyes. Everything about the stranger radiated danger, and Noble wondered why Lark couldn't see the danger that flirted so seductively before her. For even though the stranger moved and breathed and smiled within a 17 year old body, Noble noticed that his movements were those of someone or something ancient ... and evil.

The stranger leaned over and whispered something in Lark's ear. Lark was twirling a curly strand of her hair around her finger when she tensed. Everything in her expression registered panic and fear. She opened her mouth to sing, using her voice to ward off the menacing stranger and any evil, but she didn't even get the chance to scream. The stranger roughly grabbed her face covering his hand over her mouth. As he did, Noble's eyes widened as the stranger's skin turned green. He grew taller and black talons grew from the tips of his delicate, almost feminine, stick-like fingers. He held a bony, green finger to his smiling mouth, signaling for Lark to be quiet. He seemed to relish her shock and panic.

Blythe sprang up from the speaker and shoved the stranger off of Lark. The stranger stumbled backwards a few steps. The movement caused the stranger's black shades to fall from his face, and both Blythe and Lark shrank back as they noticed the stranger's glowing, red eyes. His lips curved into a wicked grin. In a movement that was almost too fast for the human eyes, the demon lunged at Blythe, sweeping his talon-tipped, fingers in a fierce slash across Blythe's chest, raking his polo shirt and the muscles and skin beneath. Blythe fell backward, his eyes widened in terror. The open gashes in his chest bled heavily, seeping into the green blades of grass. The demon licked the blood from his sharp, black talons, relishing the taste of blood.

"Mmmm," he said, closing his eyes in ecstasy.

Noble grabbed Melody by the shoulders.

"Run!" he yelled. "Get out of here!"

"What about you?" Melody asked, her own eyes wide in terror.

"I have to help my sister," Noble answered. He ran towards Lark and looked back over his shoulder at Melody one final. "Run!"

Noble ran toward Lark and the demon at a speed he felt was impossible. All that mattered was that Phony was in trouble, and he had a sinking feeling that Nick was, too. Noble felt his hands tingle as they emanated heat. He didn't need to look down at them to know that they were aglow with flames. The fire did not consume them. He aimed his hands at the tall demon as he sprinted across the field. The flame elongated into fiery blades. Noble hurled them at the demon. The fire blades cut the demon in his back and burned slowly and fiercely. The leather jacket burned first in the areas around the scorched wounds. The demon snarled in pain, releasing his grip around Lark's throat.

Lark rubbed her throat and gasped. The demon turned to face Noble. As he did, Noble hurled more fire blades into his chest. His black tee burned, revealing his green chest and torso. The demon snarled again, this time raising his hand. Time stopped. The teens became statues of panic and fear. Only he, Noble, and Lark were able to move. He raised his right hand to block a volley of fire blades from Noble. The demon stretched out his hands toward Noble, splaying his fingers, and his black, razor-sharp talons shot from them. Two of the evil talons pierced Noble's left arm. Noble felt an overwhelming stinging and burning. Before long, the burning sensation dulled and his arm felt like lead. The demon smiled at Noble, revealing fangs on either side of his evil grin. He raised his hands again, and more black talons sprouted, replacing the ones he had shot earlier.

Noble raised his good arm, untouched by the poisonous talons, and hurled more fire blades at the demon. The demon growled again. Lark, finding her voice, began to hum, at first a barely audible soprano and then more loudly, her voice picking up momentum and volume. Her soprano became two voices, and then three, growing louder and filling the field with its wordless song. The demon growled in frustration. He picked up the ends of his leather coat and whipped it around him like a cape. The coat lengthened and billowed, snapping as it twirled around him. Before Noble could blink, the demon vanished in the night air with a loud crack. His voice lingered behind.

"There's always next time," the demon said. His evil chuckle hang in the air until it, too, vanished. The motionless teens resumed their flight in various directions, scrambling to run away to nowhere in particular in their panicked escape. Noble ran to Lark, who still cast her song into the night air as she bent over to check Blythe. With gentle hands, she stroked Blythe's face. Blythe reached out to her and grabbed her arm with bloody hands before he fell unconscious.

Her arms and dress smeared in blood, Lark nodded to Noble, showing him that she was alright. She pulled out her cell phone and mimed to a nearby, wide-eyed girl to dial 911. The wordless melody spoke of safety and peace to calm the terror struck kids.

Noble felt an incredible guilt. His mind slipped to Melody and her

103

warm kiss. *How could I have allowed myself to feel even for one brief moment?* The kiss had cost him his vigilance, this scene of horror, and maybe even Nick. A sharp scream from the far side of the field cut through his guilt. The voice sounded oddly familiar as Noble ran to it, his heart sinking again into his stomach, hoping against hope that it wasn't who he thought it was.

Melody.

Noble followed the shrieking cries to the edge of the field near the forest. The kids ran helter-skelter, scattering in confused circles. Noble heard deep, guttural growls that sounded as if they came from a very large animal, but when he located the source of the growling, he was not prepared for what he saw. Hairless hounds with bones that protruded beneath their skin padded impatiently around Melody and another terrified girl. Like skilled predators, the hounds had alienated the two of them from the rest of the screaming students and cornered them against the forest opening. The two girls clutched each other, trembling and terrified at the hounds closing in before them. The other girl buried her face into Melody's shoulder as Melody warily looked on. Her lovely face was a mask of fear and unbelief. Noble studied the hounds' faces and gasped at what he saw. The faces were grotesque mockeries of humans. Rows of teeth crammed into an ill-formed maw. Their fiendish mouths hanged open in perpetual leers. The hounds snarled and snapped at the retreating girls who cried and whimpered as they withdrew farther and farther away from the crowds and into the black woods.

Their eyes glowed red, and drool trickled from their fangs burning holes into the grass beneath them. A robed figure appeared from the Whispering Woods. The hood hid its face from view. Noble was able to see clawed, scaled hands extending from either end of the robe's sleeves. Within the hooded depths of the hood, also glowed red orbs. The demon spread its arms wide and Melody and the other girl collapsed upon the ground unconscious. As Noble glanced at the girls, he noticed that Melody's orange sundress was ripped and torn. He nearly sank to his knees when he thought that she might be hurt. The demon raised its clawed hands, and Melody and the other unconscious girl floated off the ground.

Until that moment, Noble had been too shocked by the spectacle of the demon and the hounds to move. He charged in, running towards the hounds and the demon, raising his own hands. Noble felt the warmth emanating again from his fingertips. He hurled an orb of fire at the hounds. The orb scorched one hound's left flank, and it snarled and turned around to attack Noble. The hound charged at Noble at a speed impossible for a normal dog, and lunged for him. Noble had just enough time to hurl another fire orb. The orb caught the hell hound head on. The hound fell from the air mid-lunge, crashing on the ground upon its side.

Noble hurled another orb at the second hound. He missed. After dodging the fire orb, the hell hound ran back to the hovering, unconscious girls and pulled an invisible chord from the air into its jaws. An invisible sack closed around the floating girls, shielding their unconscious forms from view. The hell hound ran with the sack of unconscious victims to its demon master, who took the chord from its maw and the invisible large sack with its hidden treasure of the victim. The demon opened its robe and stuffed the huge sack, a seemingly impossible feat, within the folds of his robe. The robe must have held some curious, evil power for the sack and the girls disappeared within the folds.

Noble hurled more fire orbs at the demon. The demon waved them off with a flick of its scaled hands. He turned and studied Noble briefly, intensely. The hound that had crashed to the ground sprang back up and lunged again at Noble. Before Noble could strike it again, the hound locked its jaws around his leg. Noble felt the sharp fangs tear into his flesh and muscle. The evil hound bore down and Noble screamed. Noble poured the full might of his fire power into the hound. The hound shrieked and shivered, burning into a pile of ashes. The cloaked demon and the remaining hound fled to the edge of the field and disappeared into the Whispering Woods. The Dark now had six victims, and Melody and Nick were gone.

12

'Stolen' Answers and Nick Changed

N ick and Melody's kidnappings, Abe's disappearance, the failed attempt of protecting the students at the party, and always seeming to be three steps behind the Dark, weighed heavily on Noble. Noble and Lark wandered around their house on Azalea Street like mute zombies. They did not speak. They did not sleep. Eating became more of a mechanical action than a true enjoyment of food. They ate to keep Genesis from worrying more, doing their best to ask for seconds and pretending the food provided a temporary reprieve from their tears and worries. And even though the meal was one of the best fried pork chops, macaroni and cheese, collards, and peach cobbler Genesis had ever cooked, Noble and Lark tasted the panic and sadness she carried in her heavy breast. And Genesis sensed their fear and desperation. It was a joyless meal, quite different from the lively dinners they usually ate.

Noble knew he had to do something. He just didn't know what that something was. When Genesis learned of Nick's kidnapping, she reacted in between alarm and trepidation. She felt like she had lost one of her sons, taking out her frustration in the furious, cleansing and scrubbing of the house. The house had never been as clean or as sad. She forbade Lark and Noble from leaving the house for any reason, not even to attend school. Noble knew that he needed to look for Nick and Mr. Abe. Genesis yelled at them to stay in the house, and when Noble tried to explain she melted in a fit of hysterics, her voice rising decibels above even Abe's voice when he was in anger. It scared them, and it reminded Noble of just how powerful a Luminary his mother really was. The sky and the ground rumbled. Books, tightly wedged into their spaces on the many book shelves, pried free. Even a dark storm covered the rays of the sun. Genesis was powerful yet wounded in her love and fear for Noble and Lark. She was frantic over Nick's disappearance. She walked around mumbling to herself about nothing.

"Two drops of vanilla behind each ear will bring your beloved home. The sweetness of my kiss upon his lips. He will come home. He will come home and put this right. Not Noble. He is not ready…"

"What am I not ready for Momma?" Noble asked. Genesis grabbed him close and hugged his neck.

"Nothing, my Darling," she said. "Absolutely nothing… But don't you and Lark ever leave my sight. You hear me?" she asked. Her hold around his shoulders had tightened. His arms began to hurt.

"Okay, Momma," Noble said. "Can you please tell me what we have to be afraid of? Just tell me the truth…. Momma?"

Genesis jumped and stormed out of the kitchen, slamming the door. The wall blessing, pictures, all of her potted plants and flowers and herbs shook, and some fell. Noble had NEVER seen his mother hysterical, and it affected him in ways that he could not explain.

For days, they wandered the house in silent gloom. Noble had the sinking feeling that all of the kidnappings and disappearances, all of the random violence, the green demons who attacked at the party, were all somehow connected to his mother. He didn't know how. And he was going to find out.

There were six kidnapped victims so far, and the Darkness had promised the Blood of Seven before it would reign havoc on hearth, beginning with a foothold in Salvation. Noble was beside himself with worry. More than anything he missed Nick, he missed Abe, and more often than not, he began to think of his father. He kept wondering what his father would do in this situation and wished desperately that he was here to guide him. The Tear had not shown itself since the training session with Abe, and it didn't even appear when the demons had attacked them at the party.

Just then, his mother bustled out of the kitchen with a golden, sunflower oven mitt in one hand and a slotted spoon in the other.

"Dinner's ready, Love," Genesis said. "You and your sister go wash up and help me set the table." As he looked at his mother, dark circles showed under her eyes, and her limp was more pronounced. She shifted the oven mitt to underneath her arm and absently rubbed her hip and knee. Noble could tell that that she was in greater pain, but she was trying to hide it. Someone or something beyond Nick's disappearance made her worry. He made plans to get inside her room at the earliest opportunity to find out.

"Okay, Momma," Noble said. He ran upstairs to wash his hands and tell Lark, thinking of a time when he could go snooping.

Opportunity presented itself later that afternoon. His mother had taken Genesis into town for her piano lesson, and she warned him not to leave the house unless he wanted to attend the lesson, too. Of course, that was the last thing he wanted to do, so he agreed to stay put. With a wary glance and more pronounced limp, she left him. Before Lark left, she looked at him with quizzical eyes.

Later, Noble said in her mind. *I have to check something out, Phony… Don't worry. I won't leave the house. Go along so you don't worry Mom. I'll tell you later.*

Lark nodded, taking up the instruction books and sheet music from the piano in the den. They left.

Noble really didn't need the calced pathos, the shoes that allowed one to literally step into another's shoes and see his memories or dreams. Not anymore. Lately, all he had to do was barely touch someone's belongings or lightly brush against one's person or clothing, bump shoulders and there he was, lost in another memory, again. Just today, he touched his father's dress uniform jacket, not intending to evoke a memory, but merely trying to relive one of his own. Instantly, he was transported to his parents' bedroom six months before his father departed to a conversation they were having. At first the images were distant and dim, and the memory roiled and riled, bristled and shimmered. The images settled, revealing his mother ironing the navy sleeve of the uniform jacket he held just moments before. His father, tall and lean, came up behind her and gently removed the iron from her hand.

"You *don't* want me to iron your uniform?" she asked, eye brow raised. She folded her arms across her chest.

"You never could iron, Gen," he said. He looked into her eyes and gave her a playful smile. "You know I do the ironing and the washing and the dusting…" Genesis punched his arm.

"Besides, look at all these wrinkles. Do you want to have me court-martialed?" He pressed the uniform with determined, careful strokes. In between each one, the iron steamed and sighed.

"I suppose not," she answered. "Who would do the ironing and the dusting and the cleaning?" And then quietly, "I'd rather you not go at all." Instantly, she regretted her words. Her face became a contortionist's exhibition, an impossible oil and water mixture of fear and desperation and pride. It hinted at her unspoken need and silent joy.

She answered, "Me and the kids, we'll be all right, Aro." She squeezed his free hand.

It was his duty to go, although a small part of him cringed at the idea of leaving his wife alone with her illness and two, torrential teens, Luminaries no less. Guiding them to hone their abilities and keep their powers secret would be difficult enough, but Noble would soon face his Trial. He'd been grooming his son for this moment for years, not knowing he'd have to abandon him just when he needed him most. Besides, every Light Worker knew that the time right before a Fledgling's Trial was when male Light Warriors were most conspicuous to the Darkness. By openly helping Noble, he endangered himself and the rest of his family. And then there was Lark's hormonal upheaval which made her reckless at times as a Handmaiden of Light and his wife's illness, when after months, years of good health, had become more severe....

Noble had never heard his father speak these fears. It was strange to be made privy to his father's most innermost thoughts.

Instead Aro answered, "You'll be all right, Gen." He put down the iron and unplugged it, taking care to face the hot, metal surface away from his wife.

He pulled his wife into the sanctum of his arms and held her tightly, held her close. Aro kissed the tears on her cheeks and bent his head to cover her soft lips with his own. He hoped that his embrace and kiss could reassure her of the upcoming danger when his words and impotent actions, however well-intentioned, could not. As their lips touched, smoldering embers escaped beneath their closed lids. It was part of the wonder-working mystery that existed between them as a man and woman, husband and wife, Flame-bearer and his enchanted bride--splendorous, miraculous, and magical. The smoldering embers grew, burst into flame, and consumed them. They were not burned.

Noble turned away from them, the memory, and their love. The memory flickered and vanished. He blushed at their intensity, even after 19 years of marriage. He felt like an intruder even though it was only a memory. He began to understand something of the mystery that existed between a man and woman. He and Lark often teased or laughed at the spectacle of the smoldering glow that sparkled beneath their parents' closed door, but secretly he prayed that he would one day claim a bride of Light and know something of the mystery for himself. After tearing his glance away from this parents' golden moment, Noble reached into the bag containing the calced pathos that Abe had given him; he had to find out more. He didn't trust his own hit or miss abilities with seeing past memories. He needed to be certain.

Noble knew he was traveling in dangerous territory. To use the gift of "calced pathos", the fantastical gift that allowed one to literally "walk in another person's shoes", was an invasion of privacy. And in this case, it was an invasion of his mother's privacy, "a no man's land" if there ever was one. But a nagging and irresistible curiosity urged him on. Looking over his shoulder, he closed his mother's bedroom door and took the weathered, leather and straw sandals out of his back pack. He tugged and kicked off his new sneakers. He had to be quick. There was no telling when Lark, who couldn't keep a secret to save her life, would return from piano practice, and he did not want to waste any time. He placed first one foot and then the other into the crude thong sandals, and as Abe Cedarian had instructed, placed them in turn into the nearest shoes he could find in his mother's room.

Instantly, wondrously, his mother's smaller, sensible, blue leather pumps stretched and wrangled to accommodate his much larger feet. He took a deep breath, not really knowing what he'd find. Before he exhaled, a violent fatigue ceased him. Powerless to the vision and the feelings, perceptions, and impressions his body felt, he surrendered to the experience. Weariness. A bone weary exhaustion pulled on his limbs. His mother limped into the front office and rounded the corner to the Assistant Principal, Cypress Bane.

"Have you discovered anything?" Genesis asked him.

"Nothing yet," Cypress answered.

"Are they in any danger?" Genesis pressed him. "Does Noble have a chance?"

"There's always danger, Genesis, when one battles against the Dark." Cypress said. "He trains with Mr. Abe who helps him discover his strengths. The boy is quite talented, though I fear it will not be enough to fight against it. There's always a chance. There's always hope."

"And what of Aro? Have you seen him?" Genesis asked. She sank into the chair in front of his desk and wrung her hands.

"I'm so worried, Cypress." Genesis said. "What if they die?" She cried into her hands and Cypress took her into his arms and held her.

Noble pulled himself away from that memory and was seized again by another one, his mother walking to her classroom. She wore a black skirt and a silk, striped blouse that tied in a bow around her neck. She stumbled in the quiet morning, an hour before the homeroom bell.

Genesis trudged down the hallway at his school. Each step was like plodding, slogging through quick sand, plodding through quick sand with heavy weights. Each step was agonizing tread across icy blades, a tread across burning coals. He felt the sickly, cold sweat that lined her brow, and without warning the chee-wee-chee-wee attacked.

First long, dagger-like claws sliced through the tender muscles, his mother's muscles. Her legs, now his legs, her buttocks, their buttocks and arms, the expanse of their thighs felt as if they were being ripped from her frame. And then the gnawing began. A mere suggestion rendered her, rendered him, nauseous, and then stronger and stronger it grew. If it were a pulsing pain or perhaps a pounding, it would have been more bearable, but the chee-wee-chee-wee yielded no such mercy of predictability. The gnawing, the feasting, the gorging was all encompassing and irregular in its onslaught. Muscles and bone, joints and appendages, her head, his head, her back, no his back, her spine, now his spine, their very toes curled in agony. His mother leaned against the wall as she struggled to suppress a wave of nausea and pain.

Mercifully, it seemed as if the onslaught abated. But that was how the chee-wee-chee-wee attacked its victims, first giving them a brief respite from the torment, a small hope that the gnawing, the feasting, the gorging would stop, but then wave after wave would attack again and again and again. His mother staggered in the deserted hallway, mumbling and crying, whining and begging, trying not to attract attention to herself, but stumbling and paining and being tormented still.

Noble ran to his mother's bathroom and barely managed to throw back the toilet seat cover before he retched. Noble wept.

Wide-eyed and panting, Noble kicked off the shoes, but not before he felt his mother's last emotion: panic. *Who will protect Noble if I can't? Who will teach him the family lessons? Who will show him how to be a man? Who will teach Lark her songs? Who will show her the secrets of womanhood and mothering? Who will look after Lark when I am gone?*

He barely managed to wipe his brow and mouth before he was seized by another memory.

His mother sat in a chair, wringing her hands in Cypress Bane's office. A faint sheen of sweat glistened on her face, brow, and neck. Her legs trembled in pain, yet she waited patiently, anxious for the news that Cypress would give.

"I sense that he still lives, but whether or not he is in *this* world or the next one is yet to be determined…" Cypress answered, leaning over her like a cat over a trapped mouse. "I wish I could give you more. I know what this worrying does to you." As he spoke he dabbed her brow and cheek with his handkerchief. Noble noted that the gesture was too intimate and … possessive. His mother was so sick with pain and worry she barely seemed to notice. As she wept, he knelt beside her. Noble turned away from his mother's pain, his godfather's calculating look, and the memory. He tasted his mother's nausea, sadness, and pain.

Later that afternoon, long after Noble cleared away the dinner dishes and cleaned up the kitchen, long after his mother had lain down to rest her aching hips and knees, he heard the heavy, brass knocker rapping on the front door. Noble descended the stairs slowly, carefully, hoping there was no more news of death and abduction. When he opened the front door, a reed thin woman, with electric blue eye shadow and other garish, clown-like makeup stood at the door with her hands held on her bony hips. She wore an asymmetrical blonde wig that contrasted sharply with deep, dark chocolate skin and a neon pink mini-skirt that clung to muscular legs. Blue press on nails and silver and blue three-inch heels completed the ensemble.

What could anyone possibly want at a time like this? From us? Noble wondered.

The more Noble studied the stranger who looked oddly familiar, the more he noticed that an Adam's apple, strong, mannish hands, hard, angular legs, and a set jaw betrayed an adolescent boy in full drag. But what shocked Noble most was that the boy in drag was none other than Nick.

Noble stood at the door for a few moments torn between total disbelief, happiness, and relief. If it had been any other time than the night after his kidnapping, the incident would have been funny. In the weird way his mind worked, as he stared at Nick, he could picture him and Nick running through the house laughing while his mother and Lark chased them with a belt in hand, playfully threatening to spank them. This was not one of those playful moments full of giggling and Nick's ear-splitting laughs. Instead, Noble noticed a hard set to his jaw and cold, steel eyes that had lost all of his child-like humor and play.

"Nick?" Noble asked, "What happened to you? We looked and looked everywhere for you. We'd thought the Darkness had taken you." At once, Nick fell into his only friend's arms and cried unabashedly without restraint. In a brief pause from crying, Nick stumbled into the doorway into Noble's arms. Noble helped him to the couch in the living room. In the most unladylike manner, Nick sat like a linebacker on the bench, his hard, knobby knees forming right angles beneath the skirt. Noble felt like he was reliving a scene from the old movie *Car Wash*, with Nick starring as its worst dressed hooker. The electric blue eye shadow Nick wore didn't make it any better. Noble ran to the kitchen to get Nick a glass of water and to find him a blanket from the hall closet.

"What happened to you?" Noble asked again, handing Nick the water and draping the blanket over his shoulders and as much of the drag clothing as he could.

"I don't know," Nick answered between gulps. "I was at the party setting up, and then all of the sudden, I was in the woods. I don't remember anything more after that. I don't remember these clothes or how I got here". Nick's eyes were glassed over as if he were reliving a nightmare.

"Glu—I mean Gloria helped me," Nick said. "She showed me the way out of the woods. He ... I mean she... I can't remember."

Noble helped Nick to his feet and half- dragged, half-supported Nick to his bunk bed in his room upstairs. He gently removed the garish clothing and gave Nick a spare pair of his pajamas. Noble flinched when he saw the slashes, ridged skin, and claw marks that grotesquely marred his back and thighs. Noble wet a sudsy cloth and with gentle hands washed the garish makeup from Nick's face and neck. He gently dabbed at the scars and wounds on Nick's skin. Noble snatched the platinum blonde wig from Nick's head and hurled it into the trash bin beside his desk. As Nick's eyes closed, he noticed a peculiar red glow beneath them, but only for a few seconds. Noble shrugged off the peculiarity to nerves and pulled the comforter over Nick's body and neck.

Noble watched as Nick fell fast asleep. Noble didn't need to see the rapid movement behind his closed eye lids to know that Nick dreamed, too. Nick's dream images became a flutter of rapidly moving scenes in Noble's mind.

Noble saw it all: a demure, tearful teen, who at first seemed frightened and vulnerable, suddenly transform into an incredibly strong and malignant creature capable of changing gender at will. Noble saw the creature force Nick's terrified and tear-stained face into the ground, and with inconceivable strength, block his escape. The evil creature yanked off Nick's jeans and boxers, and what he thought was a woman with breasts and soft curves grew a member that belonged to a male. With it, he hurt and hurt and hurt and hurt and hurt Nick over and again. Nick cried out in his sleep..."NOO!"

"Oh Nick! What happened to you?" Noble said kneeling at his bed side. Noble laid his hand upon Nick's shoulder, offering whatever comfort he could. Nick sat up and leaned on Noble, and Noble wept with him, weeping for his friend, and for the man who would always have the horror of that experience. After they wept, Noble sat up straight and stared deeply into Nick's wet eyes.

"Listen to me," Noble said. "I'm so sorry this happened. I'm so sorry I wasn't there by your side to help you. We looked and looked all over but couldn't find you. And then the Darkness attacked. It was awful, Nick. Classmates slaughtered. Melody taken. And the worst thing was not knowing where you were or what happened to you." Noble clinched his hands into fists.

"But I want to promise you something," Noble said. "It's going to be alright, Nick. "We've got you. And I won't ever let anything happen to you again. You're my best friend. My only friend."

"It's too late, Noble," Nick said.

"What do you mean?" Noble said.

"I'm already ruined. I'm---" Nick said searching the bedroom floor for a word that could fit the enormity of what happened to him. "Damaged." Nick stared at the floor with hard, cold eyes. "What that thing did to me yesterday ..... making me feel hurt and ashamed--" His voice trailed off. He searched the floor again. His face was strained in pain.

"And while it all happened, all I could think about was you," Nick said, his eyes filling with tears. His voice choked, but he continued. "Your grin, your goodness, and the crazy way you take everything in no matter how bad it looks and still manage to keep going.... That's how I think I survived, by pretending to think like you, by pretending to be you...Then I felt wrong to think about you at all while that- that *thing* was hurting me, ruining me." Nick turned to Noble with agony and torment in his eyes.

"What happened to me should never have happened to anybody," Nick said. "It's like Tinny said. I'm messed up enough as it is. My mom's ...gone, probably killed by my father who's locked away. And my own grandfather treats me like I'm some kinda' trash. And now this, violated by a demon which is something I could never explain to a counselor. They'd lock me away for sure. I might as well get the revolver Gramps keeps underneath his mattress and squeeze the trigger." Nick motioned the gesture of blowing out his brains by holding his pointer finger to his left temple and cocking his thumb.

"Some joke right?" Nick asked crying again unabashedly, his tears making steady streams down his face. While Nick talked, Noble remained silent, hoping that listening to him would help release the poisonous, deadly thoughts that wore on his mind, but when Nick mentioned suicide, and Noble saw the phantasmagoric figures that hovered around him breeding self-hate and shame, Noble knew he must say something.

"Nick, you are nobody's damaged goods, and taking your life would not be a joke to me at all. There are plenty of people who care for you and need you, like me your best friend. I hate what that fiend did to you, but believe me, we will destroy it so that it never hurts another soul like that again! The best news yet in this situation is that the Darkness didn't keep you, and you are still here. And you have a family, me, Phony, and Momma. We love you and will get through this… together."

Broken, haunted, and moved by Noble's kind words, Nick moved closer to Noble. He hugged him and lay against Noble as Noble sat next to him on the bunk bed, letting his head rest on Noble's shoulder. Noble felt oddly uncomfortable about the sudden, unexpected intimacy, but he tried to be patient and comforting. Whatever happened to Nick, Noble wanted him to know that they were best buds no matter what. What he wasn't prepared for, what he didn't expect happened next.

Nick lifted his head from Noble's shoulder and grabbing Noble's chin, kissed Noble fully on the lips. Noble's eyes stretched wide. He pushed Nick away and brushed his lips roughly with the back of his hand, reeling in shock of Nick's actions. He stared at Nick, going over and over again in his mind how this moment could have even happened.

"I love you, Noble," Nick said. "I've always loved you."

"Nick!" Noble said, his voice trembling. "Clue me in to the punch line, will you?" Nick did not laugh. "This is crazy, just plain crazy. This is just the attack affecting you. Remember what Abe said? "'You are a warrior, distinctly male and strong' he said. You don't have womanish feelings. I love you like a brother, Man, nothing more."

"It's more than that," Nick said. "You've always been by my side, keeping me going in spite of the all things that have happened to me, despite Gramps' meanness, despite the craziness at school."

"What about all the girls you told me about?" Noble said. He stood up and paced back and forth in front of where they sat together moments before. "What about Phony? I thought you loved her."

"I have tried to love other girls, but now that I think of it, they've never returned my feelings," Nick said. "How could I not love Phony? She's part of you. But I'm not *in* love with her. It's always been you."

Nick stood up and closed the distance between them. He tried to reach out to Noble again, this time trying to grab his hand with his own. But Noble snatched back as if he were being touched by a viper. He tried to hug Noble, but Noble pushed back with all his might. Without trying, his fire-might escaped his hands, burning Nick's chest and forever scarring his right cheek. Noble recoiled in horror at his actions. He added yet another injury to the countless scars and suffering Nick faced already.

"I'm so sorry, Nick!" Noble said. "I didn't mean to—"

"I thought we were more!" Nick said.

"You are my brother, and I do love you, but not like that Nick. I could never love you the way my dad loves my mother, like a man loves a woman any more than I could love my sister in that way. I want the kind of love that my father and mother share. I want what they have, Nick. Nothing else."

"We could have that!" Nick said. His eyes pleaded with him.

"No, we couldn't," Noble said softly. "You are right in one thing though. You and Phony are both a part of me, like my breath, but we aren't and can never be more than that, Nick. The way a man loves a woman. That is what *I* want."

"I looked to Lark only because she is a second to you," he said. Tears glistened in his eyes. And like a dark storm cloud changes the face of day, anger flashed across his face.

Nick pulled out the scimitars and advanced to Noble. Noble remained still, trusting even when Nick held one blade against his throat. The blade nicked Noble, causing blood to trickle down his throat. As Abe promised, the blades burned hot in Nick's hands, burning him because he used them against an Innocent and against a Lightworker. Noble let his arms drop at his sides, vowing never to hurt or humiliate Nick again. He had suffered too much. And he was suffering more. Noble remained still as Nick slashed at Noble's tee shirt, tearing it to ribbons.

As Noble stared at Nick, he saw a mask of pain and torment in his face and one more emotion: rejection. His eyes became smoldering crimson, and Noble saw in that instant that things would never be the same between them again. In that one look, Noble saw how Nick was destroyed, and it wasn't just because his eyes revealed that the Darkness had attacked him, making him hurt and confused. In his confusion, he reached out to Noble in a way that Noble could not return. The Darkness had consumed him, and in his rage he scrambled over the bunk bed and crashed through the window, with amazing agility and speed. The tears he never shed for anyone flowed freely. He laughed maniacally, but this time, Noble could hear Nick's uncomforted cries. Noble ran to the window and called after him.

"Nick please!" Noble said. "Come back!" He called out the window into the dark night into after Nick, and only the silence answered.

13

Elijah and the Nazarene Tear

Noble walked in the open night air, his heart and mind a whirling tempest of emotions: sadness, fear, and regret. Anger. Anger tore through Noble as he considered the pain and destruction the war against the Darkness had cost him. So many lives affected, so many lives lost, and so many more were ruined. Even though his powers grew, they didn't seem to be enough to stem the tide of destruction the Darkness caused. And the Darkness was winning. He flashed himself in between time the way Nick had shown him countless times during training and found himself in Abe's office. The familiar tic-tic-tic of the grandfather clock made the office seem emptier, especially when no other voices were there to fill it. Abe's very essence was imprinted on every inch of the room. It was comforting to feel where Abe had filled this space with his presence even though he wasn't there.

Noble searched around the office to look for some clue, some note, that maybe Abe had left him to show him what he needed to do. He still had not found the Nazarene Tear, and at any moment the Darkness could strike again. With Nick released, if not totally back, the Darkness still needed two more innocents. Noble was running out of time.

Noble let his eyes wander around the office rooms, remembering the first time he had come into Abe's office. There was no fire burning merrily in the fireplace, and Abe's favorite teapot with the rose design was cool. Noble searched among the post cards again, wondering why he had never thought to ask Nick about the places he had visited. It was obvious by the number of cards on the wall that he was a well-traveled man. As he peered among the colorful cards and pictures, he noticed one sent from Salvation, Georgia. Why would Nick have one sent from the place he had lived at for years? Noble examined the card more closely. The paper had aged yellow and brown around the edges. He examined the date, June 4, 1857. Did they even have post cards at that time? Noble removed the ancient tack that held the card to the cork board. A heavy brass, it was not like the colorful, plastic pushpins that held the other cards to the board. When he removed the tack, a yellowed photograph fell to the floor.

Noble picked up the photograph and observed a small boy no older than seven, possibly nine with huge, round, sad, brown eyes. The eyes showed an ancient wisdom and compassion that exceeded the boy's age. Even from the unclear quality of the picture, the boy seemed ethereal and otherworldly in a rough, cotton shirt, britches, and bare feet. He held a huge magnolia in his palm. A hummingbird flitted nearby, hovering delicately over the boy's palm holding the colossal bloom. Noble sank into the couch he rested on when he had first met Abe. He remembered how Abe's large, gentle hands had healed the large goose egg that could have been a concussion from the assault by Ray's gang and caused the cracked and bruised ribs to disappear. Noble turned the picture over. The name Elijah was written in a flowery handwriting. Noble studied its graceful loops and circles. With texting these days, no one appreciated the beauty of penmanship anymore. The hummingbird, the handwriting, and the peculiar boy all seemed significant somehow, miraculous.

Noble suddenly felt tired, his legs wooden. His eyes blinked heavy with sleep. He breathed slowly, allowing the intake of air to fill up his lungs, widen his chest, and soothe him. As Abe Cederian had taught him, he took in a deep breath to quell the fear and frustration in his chest and to calm his erratic breathing. He took in another breath, and then another. He closed his eyes … and conjured a memory…

Instead of the sweet aroma of the grass that floated through the open office window, a drunken humming bird that lazily hovered nearby, and the lady and love bugs, instead of the comfortable couch, the ticking grandfather clock, instead of the ancient secretary and cork board full of postcards and pictures, a polished wooden floor and rickety pews appeared. Noble gasped as the cold fireplace he sat before became the still and gentle surface of a baptism pool. He also noticed the boy, Elijah.

Elijah stood before him sobbing; he sank to his knees. His shoulders shook with each sob. Noble recognized the look in the boy's face. It was one of heartbrokenness, one of fear. It was all that Noble could do to focus on the history that played out before him. It was too painful to watch.

"Please Lord," the slave boy cried. "Please save her. If you don't save her, Lord, she'll die! I cannot live without her." Elijah wiped the tears from the end of his nose.

"Please save Ama," he said. "If I lose her, I'll have no one. No one." The memory roiled and wavered. The images and colors shifted, churned like the contents in a snow globe and resettled.

When Noble saw the boy again, Elijah sang happily to the gardenias, azaleas, and Magnolia blossoms around him. Word traveled of Elijah. An easy favorite among the gentle ladies of the plantation, he could coax the most stubborn blossoms to bloom. They spoke of his miraculous "growing hands" that made the Stone Plantation, the most prominent plantation in Salvation, a year round Garden of Eden. They spoke of his angelic voice that soothed even the fussiest infant and of his pleasing ways and gentle, brown, dove eyes.

But only his mistress knew of his more secret and special powers, his ability to heal quickly or his gifts of healing others just with a touch of his small soft palm, of his facility to read minds, and his talent of seeing the future, to warn others of impending peril and doom, and in some cases, his power to change it.

Somehow Elijah knew not to share his secret with his masters. His own mother had warned him against letting others, especially his masters, know about all of his talents when she was alive. After all, isn't what happened to Ama proof against the dangers of trusting? Elijah missed her terribly. His mother's absence was a dull, heavy ache in his bones, especially in his tender chest and stomach. It was a pain that never went away, her death.

Sometimes in the midst of trimming Mistress's roses, his heartfelt song would give way to muffled sobs. He would quickly dry away his tears and smile at Ama's presence. He felt her with him always in the cool, gentle breeze that parted the humidity and blossoms, the air thick with their soft fragrance. Sometimes he felt Ama in the rays of sunshine or the pools of sunlight that filtered through the Live Oaks. And he still kept the Nazarene Tear, his most treasured possession and most hidden, precious secret, close to him at all times to honor her memory, her sweetest smiles and kind, gentle, quiet ways. He bore his sadness patiently and alone. He smiled through his tears and bore Master's unwarranted whip and abuse with a long suffering and patience that would rival Job.

Salvation Plantation grew under Elijah's mystical presence and of course, his faith, and his watchful eye, while the Master watched and waited for an opportunity to cause him more pain. One fateful day, Elijah felt especially content that he had managed once again to win his mistress's approval. It was Butterfly Season, that sleepy, peaceful period after Indian summer when butterflies and lovebugs hovered over the butter colored fall Lantana and darted lazily in between the passersby. In spite of the late season, Salvation was still a visual feast for the eyes of rich, fall blossoms, royal indigo, the majestic gold of sunflowers, and the orange and crimson butterfly wings and blooms.

Elijah was just making crowns and wreaths of the late summer blooms to give to the Master's and Mistress's children who he could never call equal but who didn't mind playing with him as long as Master wasn't around. For the moment, Master was nowhere to be found. So the children played quietly among the vibrant, late summer blooms while Elijah sang them sweet, wordless lullabies.

"Who is your mother?" asked a five-year-old girl with golden ringlets adorning her heart shaped face and wide, questioning eyes.

Elijah hesitated. He well knew the wrong answer could easily lead to sudden, savage brutality. He answered with a practiced care

"My mother's name is Ama," he said. "She is no longer."

"Oh Elijah," little Lily answered. Her wide blue eyes were wet with tears. "Mama can be your mother." Elijah smiled sadly and sweetly. He knew to keep quiet, although even with his wisdom he could not understand how Lily had forgotten his mother so quickly. Ama was her wet nurse who had rocked and soothed her as a colicky and fussy baby many a night.

"He's already got a mother," said Paul, a sullen, red headed boy of seven. He was just as striking as his sister except for the meanness behind his cold, blue eyes. "Papa whipped her dead before putting her in the ground. Besides, she used to be our servant, just like Elijah."

"No, he's not!" Lily answered. "Elijah's family. That's what Mama says."

"He's nothing but a slave, our *property*," Paul said. "And his mother was, too, before she got herself killed."

Again, Elijah kept silent. Out of habit and survival, he ignored Paul's insults and jeers.

"But what about your father?" Paul pressed further, a smile coiling about his face like a snake. Elijah watched him closely; he was still a child, but was quickly taking on the meanness of his father, Master.

"I don't know my father," Elijah answered, which was partly true. Ama told him that his father was sold to another plantation shortly after before Elijah was born. Somehow, Elijah believed that this was not the entire truth. But instead of focusing on all the tragedy in his life, he chose to make gaiety his friend and tease and play with the children. Most of the time, this made him happy even if he had to outwit young Paul who was steadily becoming his violent father.

The only pleasure Master got was when he meted out violence and brutality. Elijah never forgot holding his Ama's broken body after Master had beaten her to death for some imagined offense. He prayed and prayed for the Father of Light to heal her, but her broken body remained still and silent. After two days, Mistress found him, embraced him, and called him her own much to the resentment of Master Elijah learned to keep a wide berth of the man who walked in anger and darkness.

"Let's pretend that my father, Master, is father to us all," Paul said. He had a mysterious twinkle in his eye that was evil and malicious.

Elijah hesitated, but finally answered, "If that is your wish, young Master Paul."

Paul had a perceptiveness that was as sharp as Elijah. As long as the Master wasn't around, he didn't see the harm in playing the game. He laced the flower wreaths and crowns around the brother and sister's heads.

Master made no secret that he loathed the way Mistress Bond treated Elijah with as much love and kindness as she treated their own children. Master Paul had a nagging suspicion that Elijah was a living reminder of a night of drunkenness, when he cornered the terrorized Ama behind the hanging laundry. He had not bothered to look at Ama again until the night that she sang to a boy from the neighboring plantation who delivered goods to Stone. He could tell the delivery boy meant to buy Ama and her son and take her away. He knew the Mistress would not refuse Ama her happiness. After he beat Ama, he made it so she would never sing for the delivery boy again. Every time he looked at Elijah, he was reminded of haunted, brown eyes, gentle eyes, ancient, knowing eyes. It was a secret that was not spoken of and Master Paul feared that his wife knew. He would have sent Elijah away, but Gardenia was so adamant and even furious that he thought better of it--for now.

"I'll start," young Paul said. "My father is King of the World, at least of Stone plantation!

Young Lily followed suit, "My father is one of the most 'portant men in Salvation."

"*Im*portant!" Paul corrected her.

Caught up in the opportunity to have fun, which came so scarcely, Elijah answered.

"My father is the strongest, shrewdest businessman this side of the South!" Elijah yelled. The children all exploded into innocent giggles, the kind that means nothing but provides blessed release to the tension they all felt around the plantation daily.

Just then, Master Paul came charging out of the bush. No one save young Master Paul knew that his father had taken to hiding and skulking about, especially around Elijah, and in the capricious and mean manner that overtakes children sometimes, he planned this scheme just so the miracle worker Elijah who garnered his mother's attention and who had his sister's easy love could get into trouble. He smiled a slow, wicked smile, and like most things, Elijah noticed his mirth at his upcoming punishment and discomfort. His back was already a raised Braille of meanness and hurt. Elijah stilled himself for the worst, but nothing could prepare him for what followed.

Master Paul charged out of the hidden bushes with a branch the size of a rifle, and beat Elijah about the face, neck, and chest. Lily ran away crying to her mother, but young Paul watched, transfixed by the violence. Already, Elijah's face and neck dripped with blood and some of the skin was torn from his forehead. But that was not enough. Master Paul tied Elijah to a makeshift cross and secured him upside down unto the contraption. He hung the crooked cross to a gnarled, Live Oak tree.

As he hung upside down, Elijah prayed for his mother and asked God if he would see her again soon, sensing that this was the end, and he prayed a feeble prayer for a quick death and the strength to keep the secret, the Tear. Through swollen eyes, Elijah looked at Master Paul. His face was a mask of savage brutality. As he lay upside down waiting for the end of his short, cruel life, Elijah passed out. When he awoke, the sun had set and the dark night covered a black sky free of stars. Elijah raised his head feebly.

His head pounded and his throat ached for water. He heard the tinkling of glasses and the sound of laughter. Elijah saw many slave masters, holding torches, swords, guns, and hot pokers. The elegantly dressed, genteel women drank lemonade and fanned themselves coquettishly to wait for the entertainment. It began.

"This idiot, worm of a slave has the audacity to refer to me as father!" yelled Master Paul. "I called you all today to make this an event that will not soon be forgotten. Each of you holds a party favor. ..." Master Paul picked up a blunt instrument from the table and waived it at the assembly. Several men cheered while the ladies fanned themselves feverishly in excitement.

"I want you to give our guest of honor a sending off he will never forget," Master Paul continued. "This animal, this no-good nigger dares to compare himself to upstanding people."

Elijah took a deep breath and sighed that the agony was not over and waited patiently for the end. The guests lined up with their clubs and their pokers and their knives like children waiting to take their turn to bludgeon a piñata. A genteel woman made a show of stabbing Elijah in the side. Elijah's blood bled freely. The next angry demon, for they could not be human beings as Ama had taught him, clubbed him over the head with a log covered in nails......

Noble passed out again long before the "party" was over, but Master Paul had other plans. Master Paul bent his face to Elijah's mouth to see if he could detect a breath. At first he could not find one, and he cursed at his luck. But at last he found a weak and shallow breath. He took heated stakes and drove them through the ankle bones and wrists of Elijah.

Elijah yelled one final, ragged shriek. The skies rumbled and there was no sound to be heard in the forest that surrounded the plantation. No crickets chirped, no frogs croaked, no hunting wolves howled. The small animals did not scamper or scurry. The wind did not blow. There was just the deafening silence.

A few of the ladies giggled nervously. They made their hurried excuses and gathered their belongings to leave. A few men shook hands and thanked Master Paul for a reminder of the "Good Ol' Days". But they made their weak, rushed excuses and left. Soon, the only one left was Master Paul and what was left of the young Elijah. Mistress had been visiting her sister for the day and returned to the display of violence in shock and silence. She held Lily closer to her and cried, rocking her in her embrace. Even young Paul had slinked back to his rooms, devastated by the prank that had gone to far. The sky rumbled louder in anger.

"You want to be a saint so bad, but everyone knows a nigger can't be no angel," Master Paul said. "Hell, niggers don't even go to heaven". Therefore, I made you an upside down cross, a crooked one, just so others would know that there is no such thing as an angel nigger!"

Elijah gave up his ghost in one last sigh. Young master Paul was stunned. Having never witnessed more violence than pulling off the wings of a butterfly, his heart pounded rapidly, he sweated, and he ran to his room and buried his face into his pillow. When Mistress Gardenia found her Elijah, not her real child, but her child in spirit none *the less*, she stared at what was left of her sweet voiced, dove eyed angel in a quiet, simmering anger. She made a promise a long time ago at Ama's death bed that she would take care of Elijah as her own, and she sank to her knees, heartbroken that she did not keep her promise. The very spirit of Gardenia and her daughter changed. They no longer smiled, spoke much, and never gathered flowers again. But days after Elijah was tortured and killed, they were both visited by him. As he stood before him, his gentle brown cheeks and brown, dove eyes unblemished and glowing as if he'd never been hurt or maimed days before, he told them not to blame themselves and that he would see them again someday.

"Thank you for being a family to me, Mistress," he said smiling at Gardenia. He touched little Lily's cheek. "The Light has other plans for me now, and I must go to do His will. I will also see Ama, and I will tell her what a great family you were to me. I promise we will see each other again." A large, single tear rolled down his cheek and grew and glistened. It floated off his face and into the air. It shimmered and began to fade away. Elijah's glowing presence followed, gradually disappearing before them. As they saw his being dissolve into the air, they were comforted that he had promised to see them again.

In the morning, the smug Master Paul went to the crooked cross to admire his handiwork and noticed that the cross was right side up, the tree it hung upon was larger and that once bare, its branches were bounteous in lush leaves. All the blood and evidence of last night's brutality had disappeared. Elijah's body was gone.

He became more bitter and unhappy, and in turn, young master Paul became unruly and difficult to handle. It was the kind of bitterness that comes from the anger of self and anger at the cruelty of others. Master Paul could do nothing to control him, until he, too, ran away.

On a dark night clear of stars and the waning light of the moon marred by thunder clouds, Master Paul visited the site where he killed Elijah. His wife and daughter left him after his son had run away. No longer the finest plantation in Salvation, all the former glory that was once Stone Plantation was gone. The house, his business, his marriage, his very life had dried up like ancient, powdered turd. He begged to any powers that existed that he could regain power, more power than he ever knew as a human, and he begged to all that was evil, that he could take his revenge on Elijah, the root, he thought, of all of his misery.

Just then, an old man with cotton hair and clear, flawless, sepia skin walked silently past Master Paul as he prayed to all that was evil since he felt that all that was good had abandoned him. The old man stopped and stared at the bitter, crying, man for minutes until Master Paul finally noticed his presence.

"I wouldn't do that if I were you," the old man said. "Any bargain made with the Darkness is a bargain made against yourself. It's a dangerous piece of business with never a happy ending. Forgive and be forgiven, Mr. Stone, while you still can."

"Shut up, Nigger!" Master Paul yelled. "Did I ask for your opinion?"

"No, but you do need forgiveness for all of the people you have wronged. Then you will know peace," The old man said. And in front of old Master Paul's eyes, the old Negro man vanished, but not before giving him a pitying look.

Noble woke up as from a dream. His body felt lighter and more refreshed, his eyes and limbs less heavy. Noble sprang up from the couch when he remembered the old man in the dreaming memory. He was Abe.

14

Crossing Over

A figure crept outside the Goodson home in the late night hour. It wrapped itself in blackest shadows, gathering the unnatural darkness around him like a shroud. The shadows were made up of a darkness that was not of this world. They made the night around them look bright like the day. The shadows unfurled, covering the area surrounding the house, blacking out the stars, and obscuring the bright moon. The center of the blackness floated just outside an open hall window upstairs. It hovered in the hallway outside the rooms of breathing forms. It paused briefly outside Lark's room, hovered menacing outside Noble's, and then picked up speed again before Genesis's partly closed door. The blackness stretched and thinned out and shrank to the size of a speck of dust. Genesis inhaled, coughed in her sleep, rolled over, and then began lightly snoring again. The snoring stopped when she began moaning and grinding her teeth, her hips and legs became one great pain. She whimpered and tossed and turned until the early morning hours. Something evil without face or form laughed softly in the dark.

A key clicked in the door. A long, roaring creak betrayed Noble's late return. Noble opened the door with anguished caution, slowly easing it back towards its frame. A louder click followed by a shower of bright, accusing light outlined Noble's surprised form and his mother's angry night-gowned one.

"Noble, where have you been?" Genesis asked. Dressed in her lilac night gown, she charged toward him. Even then, hard lines edged with illness, creased her soft and otherwise youthful face.

"Wouldn't *you* like to know?" he asked. His face revealed a mix of conflicting emotions: anger, audacity, ire, and guilt, the guilt mostly. He hated to cause his mother worry. Stress was one of her illness's triggers.

"Wouldn't I like to know?" she asked. Her words were more of a shout than question. "Boy if you don't get that disrespectful tone out of your voice --- I swear I will slap it out of you!" *Pimp-slap was more like it, Noble thought.* His mother was not a small woman, and from the few times she had spanked him and his sister he knew he did not want to provoke another beat-down, especially at 14. "It is 2:00 am on a school night -- Where have you been?" she repeated.

"I don't ask you of your whereabouts when you slink over to Mr. Bane's house, or should I call him Uncle Cypress?" He braced himself for the slap. He expected it. He deserved it. He imagined himself angrier for it somehow. Instead, his mother's silence surprised him. Silence was different. It worried him.

Genesis still towered a full foot above him. All of her height seemed to bear down upon him now. Eons of silence passed before she answered.

"When people know they are loved, they don't ever live in fear of what their loved ones can do to them," she answered. "Your father trusts me, and we've built a solid foundation over the years. Marriage, children, disappointment, joys, that kind of bond is impossible to destroy. We have an unbreakable bond. The person I don't know right now is you," she answered. Her last words were measured words, forceful, final. She left him in the silence to think about her words. He tossed and turned until the early morning thinking about them, but he thought about his own words and how he hurt her more. Soon after, he got the angry call from Lark to meet her at the hospital. His mother was violently ill.

The image of his mother lying in a hospital bed in the county hospital haunted him still. Tubes vied for claim of scant veins that lined Genesis's arms. An oxygen mask held custody of her face. Noble hated that he could no longer see her smile. He wouldn't be able to see one even if she didn't wear the mask. Genesis had been unconscious for days. The chee-wee-chee-wee was the worst he had ever seen it. Her skin, no longer a glowing, golden butter, was a pallid bisque. Her body, no longer larger than life and always in motion, seemed broken, frail, and unsettlingly still. Her face wore a perpetual grimace, evidence of the intense pain of the chee-wee-chee-wee. From a hellish pit in the Spirit Realm, millions of sinister maws ripped through space and time to ravage the capillaries, bone, and muscles of Genesis, denying her solace even in sleep.

The last words between his mother and him before she fell ill were angry words, hurtful and bitter. Soon after, she was rushed to the emergency room, and his world came crashing down.

He left Lark at the hospital with a tale that he would go home to get some of their mother's comforting belongings: scented lotions, her favorite perfume, more nightgowns and needed undergarments, her favorite brush, and the creased, dog-eared copy of her favorite novel. Lark's accusing glare chided him even when her words different:

"*I* can run home and get those things for Momma," she said. "You've done enough."

"No, I will get them," Noble said. "You stay here with her. Sing to her, Phony. She's always comforted by your voice. Sing blessings and protection until I return."

And because Phony rarely missed a thing, she asked, "Where are you going? You know Momma needs you."

"I just told you," Noble answered. "I'm going to get Momma's things." He headed to the house and just as he said, he gathered his mother's belongings. He left them with a note for his Aunt Byzantine to drop them at the hospital. He also packed a bag for himself. He tried to pack perishable items: an apple, pears, two fried chicken drumsticks, half a bread loaf wrapped in a cloth napkin and water in a flask. Why he couldn't pack aluminum foil, paper or wrapping of any kind was beyond him. He followed Abram's directions without question.

Next, he planned to rescue the Nazarene Tear as well as the Innocent. The Tear was said to hold the Savior's healing powers. If anything could save Genesis, Feeder of the poor, teacher, friend, a strong woman of the church, his mother, it would be the Tear, but in order to find it he had to Cross Over.

Noble swallowed a sob and hardened his resolve. His mother's chiding remarks haunted him: "Remember strife and fighting provide entry ways for the Enemy to penetrate…"

They had been true. Genesis was deathly ill. Noble knew the journey to the Spirit Realm was perilous. There, he could no longer pretend not to notice the evil spirits, demons, and wicked angels: they could see him as clearly as he could perceive them. And while the idea of confronting evil beings and demons in the Spirit World nearly paralyzed him with fear, the fear of living in his world, the real world or the next one, without his mother was greater still. He had to go.

Noble tried to clear his mind, and focus on the principles Abe Cedarian had taught him about Crossing Over, and how it would take an untroubled and focused mind and strong faith. He recalled Abe's rich, deep, yet gentle voice, his wisdom, and his calm. He knew he would need to focus on an object, a possession, or even an image that was a unique and distinct reflection of the person sought after, and since he sought to deliver his mother, he focused on her.

He walked around his mother's room, settling his mind. The flowers needed watering. Books were strewn across her bed and on the dresser. He picked up a copy of *Possessing the Secret of Joy*. He noticed many dog-eared pages and her scrawled comments in the margins of nearly every page. He could still feel her presence here. Noble fingered a framed family photograph. He, Lark, his mother, and his dad were frozen in a loving embrace. His father circled his mother in a protective and adoring embrace. They all laughed. He settled on his mother's smile and wry grin. He smiled at his mother's laughter. It was infectious. Gosh, he missed his father and mother. It was hard to get used to his father's sudden absence. To make matters worse, when he returned home, there was an opened letter on the foyer table. It was addressed from the National Guard.

..... regret to inform you that Sgt. Goodson is missing.....

Noble crumbled the paper in his fist. He was sure his mother and Phony had read it. Now the letter had made their deepest fears real. He felt like someone had slipped a rug out from beneath his footing. He could not, would not accept his father's disappearance. It just wasn't true. To be without his mother, too? Unbearable.

Suddenly, his gaze settled on one of his mother's paintings. It was a rendering of a sickle cell crisis by a Haitian artist Hertz Nazaire. The painting showed an infant whose mouth, twisted and agape, cried out in pain. Crescent shaped red blood cells with sharp and jagged edges surrounded a chain, an artery secured to a tortured and beating heart, locking the infant inescapably and helplessly in unspeakable torment.

Noble stood before the picture and cried out to it.

"Open!" Noble commanded. Noble barely noticed the sudden dip in temperature or the wavering in the fabric of reality. Instead, he gasped as the infant's mouth cried out, stretched and grew, wrangled to become at first an opening and then to Noble's amazement, a door. It swung inward and opened into cold darkness.

Noble peered cautiously into the darkness and paused at the threshold. He hesitated only briefly before summoning all his courage. He called out to the darkness:

I, Noble Adjani Goodson, son of Light, come to aid the Flamebearer Genesis Thessalonia Goodson, to set her free from the jaws of pain, and even from shackles of death…I come to free the Innocent, to chase back the Darkness, and to petition the Nazarene Tear.

His words echoed and rebounded and called back to him; the Blackness swirled and roiled. A cacophony of whispers and jeers and howls mocked him and beckoned him forward. He grabbed his backpack and walked through. He knew he had entered the Spirit Realm.

The air was much thinner, colder. The Blackness was not really a black at all, but an ever changing rich indigo, sepia, and inky coal. His eyes took what seemed like ages to adjust to the weak and eerie light provided by three faint moons obscured by menacing clouds. There were no stars, no breeze, no chirping crickets, or any natural sound to remind him of a normal world. And as he walked, he noticed that the ground was hard and cold. Every so often dry, withered roots cracked through stone surface. A feeling that was more intuition told him to steer clear of them as much as possible. He walked and walked. He climbed over violet boulders when he was not stepping carefully around crags and huge stones. Noble felt exposed. He felt as if he was being spied upon and he had no natural cover to hide his form. He zipped up his jacket against the cold. The wind was strong here. It carried a biting chill. In the distance he saw what looked like the base of mountains. It was hard to tell in the dim light and the wind that slapped and bit at his eyes and face. After what seemed like miles he saw the first real vegetation. Trees.

Peculiar trees of indigo and ochre and crimson barks marked what looked like the beginning of a dense copse. Unlike the beautiful and affecting Live Oaks of his home, these trees had dry withered branches that loomed forward as if trying to grab passersby. As Noble looked more closely, he could make out the remains of decomposed skeletons that hung from the most menacing limbs. A beastlike ribcage, a lone skeletal arm, and a fractured pelvis formed macabre tree ornaments. In one limb a skull leered. Its open jaws seemed stretched in a final and silent scream. He kept a safe distance from them. After a second thought, he crept and edged closer to the trunk of one of the crimson trees. He felt oh so carefully for the surface of the bark. Instead of a smooth or rough surface, these barks were spongy. Noble felt like the time he cleaned the mold from underneath the old refrigerator in Mrs. Sphinx's house. Noble craned his neck upward as he observed the heights of the trees to go up and up forever.

Noble jumped when he heard the sound of foot falls. Something huge and monstrous was coming. Its rhythmic gait pounded the stone surface, dislodging small rocks and pebbles. It trudged through the strange woods and it was coming closer, closer to him. He ducked behind the wide trunk of the indigo tree, pressing his body flat against its bark and hoping that he wasn't spotted. Just then, a withered root broke through the hard ground, followed by another. They snaked across the hard, craggy ground and found his left ankle and his thigh. They held him to the spot. Other roots burst through and lunged for his arms. He struck out at them, dodged them. The footsteps pounded closer. His heartbeat pounded like an anvil, and the footsteps pounded closer still. They were less than half a mile now, and if he wasn't hidden behind a few trunks, he knew he could see what made them. He knew what made those heavy footsteps would also be able to see him. It would be any minute now before they discovered him.

He cast about in his mind for some wisdom or advice that Abe had given him, something that would help him. He suppressed an urge to scream, knowing perfectly well if he betrayed his presence this soon after Crossing Over, he would never be able to help his dying mother. He also knew now what happened to the unlucky skeletons and how they had become tree ornaments. He did not want to be one. Just then, he remembered. Before his last training session with Abe had ended, the Wise One had given him seeds. Mustard seeds he called them. Abe said that with just a little faith they would accomplish much. Noble dug his hands in his jeans pocket to find them. He fished out one just as another root grabbed at his left hand. With a small prayer he dropped one in the earth below and wished for sanctuary. First nothing. And then a mighty rustling, rumbling quaked beneath. Branches erupted, burst through the dry ground, followed by a huge tree. Because he knew he had to have faith, he tried not to feel a sinking feeling when he mistook the branches for roots. Next, the violet trunk emerged. The tree had a large, gaping mouth and branching hands. It reached down, grabbed at Noble and swallowed him whole into Darkness. Noble fell hard and would have hurt himself if something soft did not soften his fall. Grass! Soft, springy, crimson grass! Noble started to cry out in triumph when he was silenced by a small, but meaningful "Shhh". Noble looked around for a body but found one.

"Shh!" It repeated again. "Peer quietly out of the spy-hole," it spoke again. "But whatever you do, be silent!"

The voice was decidedly feminine, like a chiding school teacher. Noble followed quietly. He found a very small, very inconspicuous hole that served as a spy-hole. Outside he found what made the thundering footfalls and nearly jumped when he saw large behemoth beings with the muscular and hairy bodies of a men and the heads of boars sniffing about where Noble had been only moments before. Their large snouts wavered in the air and circled the tree several times. Upon discovering no prize they began to pound onward and beyond. Noble spied the back of one hairy retreating form. Its arms hung well beyond its knees, and from huge, powerful hands, long talons skimmed the ground.

As far as he knew, he wasn't discovered. Noble sighed.

"Didn't I tell you to be quiet," the voice hissed again. This time Noble was determined to find its owner. Reassured that danger had passed, the voice revealed itself. A dim light grew stronger to reveal a woman's face in the wall of the tree's very large hollow.

"Make yourself at home, Son of Light," she said. Noble searched around and found wall papered interior, inscribed names of previous Light Warriors, a comfortable straw bed, antique looking skins of wine and hanging wheels of bread and cheese. The place looked homey, if you could call a tree hollow a home.

"What?" Noble cried.

"Didn't I tell you to be quiet?" the face hissed again. "At least lower your voice. And I was told you were one of the bright ones, 'one of the most promising'. Just goes to show you. Can't listen to everything you hear."

"How did I get--- Am I still in the Spirit Realm?"

"You called and I answered. It's as simple as that. You needed sanctuary. You used the mustard seeds. You had a little faith. Here I am," she said.

"Huh?" Noble said.

"Many have called, and I always answer. Why don't you settle down and rest until you can plan your next move. It's tricky here, very tricky. You're going to have to have your wits about you if you plan to rescue the Innocents and save your mother."

Noble nodded and yawned. He hadn't noticed how tired he really was. He must have traveled for hours. Suddenly, the straw pallet on the bed looked very comfortable, very comfortable indeed. His eyes were heavy and his ankle, wrist and shoulders ached from the dangerous roots.

"Help yourself to the bed and the wine and the cheese. You can stock up on your provisions if necessary. I wouldn't eat all of your food all at once. There's water here also. I'll be here as long as I'm needed, but it will be best if you clear out by next night. Those oafish pig-for-brains aren't cunning, but they aren't exactly stupid either. They'll be back. It would be best if you and I weren't here when they return. I'll awaken you. By the way, my name is Lady Ash."

Noble nodded again. He plopped down on the straw bed without removing his shoes. He was that tired. He pulled off the backpack and took out the two drumsticks. He drank from the wine flasks Lady Ash had given him and ate of the bread, too. As advised he packed more of the wine, bread, cheese, and other provisions into his backpack.

The passing monsters were one type of the Darkness's sentries. Noble was beginning to trust an inner discernment that advised him that though he was unfamiliar with this world, that when the three moons aligned they would give out a stronger light, and more sentries would be patrolling the realm. He knew that he would be more visible once this happened. He was grateful he had a place to hide. Noble could now understand why Abe had instructed him to wrap his food with cloth napkins that he needed to carry with him. After glimpsing his surroundings, he knew that a discarded wrapper or soda can would signal his arrival. Noble did not want company.

He pulled out the old, mystical slave quilt that doubled as a map and wrapped it around his body to ward off the chill. He knew he could not start a fire for warmth in this place. He was afraid of what the welcoming flames would attract. Besides, he didn't want to hurt his fussy tree friend. He might need her help later on. He thought he would never fall asleep as he waited for the moons to grow dim again. Just as he dozed off, Noble was jolted awake by a large, gentle hand that covered his mouth. He was too scared to scream, even beneath the huge hand, until he noticed that a soft, gold light emanated from the stranger's other hand. Its finger raised itself to the stranger's lips to signal silence. On its ring finger, he recognized a thin wedding band. In the soft, glowing light, Noble made out the bronze skin, white cotton beard, but most of all, the gentle brown eyes of his friend.

He threw his arms around the hooded form of Abe Cedarian.

"You came," he whispered.

"I came," Abe whispered back. "I couldn't let my best pupil face the Darkness alone".

15

Help from a Long Lost Friend

"I have so much to tell you!" Noble said. "Where have you been? What happened to you? Didn't you hear us calling you?" Did you find out anything else about the Tear?" Noble's words came out in an excited rush.

"There's a chatty one!" the Lady Ash said.

"One question at a time," Abe answered, his eyes sparkling and clear as he smiled.

"What happened?" Noble asked. "We've been trying to find you, trying to reach you for days!"

"Yes," Abe answered. "I heard you. I'm sorry I couldn't answer, but as you may have already suspected, my identity as a Luminary has been compromised. I was …. detained."

Noble bit his lip, worried about what Abe's blown cover may mean to him and to their friendship. Would he see him again? As with every situation, Abe answered with a smile.

"I was --" Abe said pausing, "We were being watched. I'm sorry to say that we have a traitor in our midst."

Noble's thoughts immediately shifted to Cypress. His eyes were too shifty, his motives too shadowed, and his intentions too hidden to be trusted. Noble had long suspected that his godfather may not have been on the right team.

"Careful Noble," Abe answered. "Some things aren't always what they seem."

How could he not suspect him? Noble thought about how he had come to Cypress's office, practically begging him to cancel the party to prevent more bloodshed and kidnapping and that Cypress, who had been trusted to protect the students of the school but also precious life as a Luminary, had refused. It simply did not make sense. But because Noble had learned to trust Abe and value the Wise One's opinion, he kept his doubts at least unspoken though he well knew that with Abe he could not hold any secrets.

"Who then?" Noble asked, wishing he had the power and permission to probe Abe's mind.

"Patience," Abe said. "All will be revealed. I am sorry that I did not answer when you called. It was very difficult to hold back and to remain silent when you faced such danger. I am proud to see that Salvation was in very capable hands. You are indeed Salvation's Champion, Noble. I never doubted it." As Abe spoke Noble saw that Abe's eyes glistened in tears.

Noble's heart swelled with gratitude and admiration.

"Thank you, Abe," Noble said. "I didn't feel like anyone's champion. Half the time I was running scared and the other half I didn't know what to do. I've made so many mistakes, Abe. And Nick--" Noble's voice choked as if the words he meant to speak caught in his throat.

"What leader doesn't make mistakes?" Abe asked. "It is how a person learns from his errors that determine how strong a leader he will be." Again, Abe's eyes glistened with sadness in the pale light.

"I feel your loss, Noble," Abe said. "For as you see Nick as your brother, I want you to know that I consider you both my sons. I must shoulder much of the blame. I had not considered that either of you would be attacked so viciously. I tried to prepare you both for battle, but one never knows for certain how and when the Darkness strikes."

"But Nick thinks –" Noble said. "Nick's not …. himself anymore. And it's all my fault!" Noble's eyes looked darkly, glistening with tears.

"The Darkness searches for weaknesses," Abe said. "Nick's weakness wasn't his identity. It was his sore need for the love of his father or any adult male figure who cared for him. Nick didn't have that. The Darkness saw that and brutally exploited it."

Noble looked away from Abe, his eyes dark, and his head swimming in questions. *Will Nick ever be the same again? Will Nick heal? What are my weaknesses?*

"The Light never makes an error. As I said, Nick is a warrior, male, strong, and true. One of the weapons of the enemy is confusion. Because Nick has a destiny, it attacked him. Just as it attacks you. Can you not think of your weakness or rather your strength?"

My family and friends! Noble thought. He pictured all the faces of the loved ones in his circle who were attacked: *Piccolo. Melody. Nick. Momma….Dad.*

"Is that why they suffer?" Noble asked. "Because of me?"

"That and their association to the Light. To Goodness and their potential," Abe said, his eyes sparkling. "But now we must get some rest while we can. We have a battle before us and we might not get this opportunity again."

Noble hunkered back down under the old slave quilt, his mind buzzing with more questions and thoughts. Abe sat down beside him, his head atop a large, soft root that served as a coarse pillow. He folded his hands over his chest and drifted off to sleep. Noble threw one end of the quilt over Abe's dozing form and the other end over his head. He closed his eyes. Before long, he drifted off to sleep.

16

Two to the End

Noble woke to the sound of whispered voices and packing. He heard Nick's low tones conversing with the tree. Noble stood up and rubbed his aching back and legs. His wrists and ankles were still sore from the attack of the roots. He opened one of the flasks and tasted the sweet water. He held his head back and let the sweetness wash over his tongue and throat. He rubbed the sleep from his eyes.

"I believe that is as much as we can carry," Abe said.

"No more water?" the tree asked. Wine and water skins, blankets, and loaves of bread stuffed themselves into the bags. "What about wine? You don't know how long it will be before you come upon fresh water again, and the wine can be used for cleansing wounds as well as calming nerves."

"Perhaps more water for the boy," Abe said.

"For the boy?" the tree asked. Noble could hear the tree branches and leaves bristling as if with anger. "He already has twice as much as you now. You pack as if only one of you will return--"

"There is our waking Champion now," Abe said. "Are you well rested?" Abe's eyes twinkled again.

"A little," Noble said. In truth, Noble had tossed and turned during the few hours of rest allowed. He snatched moments of sleep between night terrors and fitful moments of positioning his aching neck, back, and shoulders. He was a wreck.

Abe rested his large palms of Noble's shoulders. A rush of warmth and peace flowed through Noble's aching limbs and muscles and calmed his anxious breathing, upset stomach, and erratic heartbeat. Noble felt …. good. He wondered if the sick who sought his mother's healing felt the same.

"Better," Abe said. "Your mother's ability to heal others is part of her calling to the Light. Her efforts bring many believers to the Light. It is a tragedy that Genesis is unable to heal herself, but that is part of her path that will be revealed in time.

Noble thought of his mother's hurting limbs. He frowned as he thought of the Live Oak's words: *"… only one of you will return…"*

Abe waved at Noble, gesturing for him to join him in a humble breakfast of bread, cheese, and cool water.

"Sit," Abe said. This time Abe's twinkling eyes seemed lit from within. Another tree root served as a rough table and chairs. Noble sat in one chair as Abe sat on the other.

"Fear is one of our greatest weaknesses," Abe said, tearing a golden brown loaf in half. "It undermines our ability to believe. This may be the last opportunity for me to offer any instruction or advice. So please listen closely…"

Noble nodded and leaned closer. He munched on a wedge of cheese. It had surprisingly, nutty flavor.

"What is the first thing you should do when approaching any agent of the Darkness?" Abe asked.

"Clear your mind," Noble said into Abe's mind. Noble imagined a white water basin, filling with cool, rustling water. The surface rippled and bubbled. He projected the image into Abe's mind.

Good, good, Abe said. *Don't limit your imagery.* Abe projected cleansing water in various ways: a small, babbling brook, a roaring waterfall, a rushing stream, the crash and roar of the ocean.

Noble saw each of these images clearly.

"No matter what form the Darkness appears in, no matter how it threatens, you must always operate from this peaceful state. The Darkness distracts. The Darkness deceives. The Darkness destroys. It takes great pleasure in killing, in crushing hopes.

Noble thought of all the innocent lives that were taken and the wake of destruction left behind in its carnage and violence.

"What forms has the Darkness taken to hurt and kidnap its victims?" Abe asked.

Noble thought of the seductive, pale green, black haired twin brother and sister that frequented his dreams and attacked at the party. He shivered when he thought of the hounds with the man-like faces and the hooded stranger with clawed, monstrous hands.

"Those evil hounds that you saw are hell hounds. The deadly, lascivious twins are Lust and Envy. They all serve a more ominous Dark Agent, Ba'al. Those grotesque canines are his pets, Glut and Glomit. What I've been pondering is how they have been able to grow so strong and attack in our realm. While the hounds gorge on human flesh, Ba'al and his servants feed on fear. The kidnappings and attacks aren't enough to keep them in this world. Someone, although maybe unwittingly of our order has been giving them a steady diet of worry and fear. Only someone with the powers of the Light could sustain a force that powerful."

Noble sucked in his breath. The color left his face and he felt his heart sink to his stomach. *Who else had been frantic with worry since he became of age? Who else had allowed fear to trigger the chee-wee-chee-wee which had been dormant for years? Who had spoken against him at his trial, hoping to steer him from the dangerous path as Champion and Luminary?*

"Oh, Momma!" Noble cried. He sank to his knees, his legs heavy with the gravity of his revelation. He was heartsick that his mother loved him so much and that her love had cost her well-being, had cost Salvation so much. What had Abe said? 'The Darkness used family ties and affections against those in the Light.' His mother, a high ranking Luminary, was not immune. She had suffered much for him and was still suffering. The Darkness fought ferociously, and they fought for keeps.

Abe stared intently at Noble, kindness and sympathy showed in his eyes.

"When you fight against the Darkness, you will have to put all thoughts of any person you love, Lark, Nick, your mother, your father, even me, out of your mind," Abe said. "Do you understand?"

Noble shook his head mutely.

"The Darkness has studied your fighting," Abe said. "He knows of your Firemight. He knows what makes you angry. I would not be surprised that the Darkness has not already developed a way to rid your firemight ineffective against his agents. You will have to search deeply within yourself to call forth the mighty, new weapons needed to defeat them."

"A new weapon?" Noble asked. "What exactly could that be?" He wasn't prepared for this fight. He'd never practiced for this.

"Remember, your worst enemy is not the Darkness, Noble," Abe said. "It is your fear and doubt. Fear and doubt limit you in ways that will prove fatal. Think boldly! Dare to conjure in your mind beyond what you are normally capable of. The firemight, the mustard seeds, these are only the beginning of your untapped power. Your potential is far greater...."

"Are you ready, Lady Ash?" Abe asked.

"I am ready," the tree responded. Noble heard a great rumbling. The tree quaked and shook as a great root erupted and grew in size. Soon the root had become a large tunnel. Abe shouldered his bag and grabbed a staff made of dried roots. It was agile and strong, quivering with power, like Abe. Noble slipped his bags on his back as he marveled at the huge, root tunnel.

"This tunnel takes you to the foot of the mountain near Ba'al's lair," the tree said. "There is where you will find the Innocents. Will this really be the last time, Abram?"

"Only in this realm, Lady Ash," Abe said. Abe smiled and laid his hand upon the surface of the tree's wall. Where he placed his hand the figure of a woman emerged. Her hair was a thick mane of leaves and branches and her skin was the smooth bark of the tree. The woman opened her eyes and stared lovingly at Abe.

"I will always love you, Abram," the tree said. "From the day, you bled freely on my trunk."

"And I you, Lady Ash," Abe said.

17

Against the Darkness

N oble trekked through the root tunnel in silent determination. Abe followed behind closely in long, measured strides. They had each donned hooded robes to help mask their identity.

Although, their inherent goodness, Abe warned, carried a unique scent easily detected by any servant of the Dark, especially Hell Hounds. Abe also warned him to communicate only through their thoughts and to do so sparingly. Although the root tunnel was several feet beneath the surface, Noble could tell they traveled deeper and deeper into the Darkness. Noble struggled to breathe in the thick, rank air. Farther back in the tunnel, there were more roots and blades of grass. Here the walls of the tunnel root were bare and dry. And the air smelled putrid and rotten … like corpses. The stench burned the back of his throat and nostrils. Abe took out a skin of water and took a long drink before passing it to Noble. Noble drank deeply, allowing the cool water to soothe his throat.

The air was thick with danger, and the silence was deafening. Ahead of him, the darkness thinned. Noble's eyes adjusted in the dim light. The tunnel ended. An opening overhead permitted the weak light of the three moons. Suddenly the tunnel slanted upward, causing their pace to slow to an upward crawl.

Stay alert, Abe spoke into Noble's mind.

Noble nodded, fighting a compulsion to turn around and run back.

Wait, Abe said, speaking into Noble's mind. He placed his arm across Noble to block him from climbing up. Abe closed his eyes and concentrated. His physical contact with Noble allowed Noble to see what Abe was seeing. Noble looked down as from an aerial view. Thorny bushes masked a hole in the stony ground. Here and there barren trees with branches that resembled outstretched arms broke through the hard ground. A scattering of boulders marked the entrance to a large cave, resembling a wide, gaping maw, which receded into the side on an inverted mountain. The very bottom, an inverted apex, marked the lair of the Darkness.

Just then a black, three foot beetle, larger than the roaches that attacked him on the bus ramp, hovered over the opening. It snapped its pinchers and waved its stinger waiting. Its quivering form hovered back and forth across the opening.

What the --? Noble thought.

Sentry Beetles, Abe said. *A special guard of the Darkness.* Abe waited. As soon as the quivering beetle breached the opening, Abe struck out with the staff made of gnarled roots. A short burst of light hit the huge beetle, burning a whole clean through it. The beetle fell through the opening of the tunnel with a thud. The fire continued to consume the giant bug until it was only a pile of ashes. Abe shot through the tunnel opening in a single bound, nimble in spite of his age.

Is this where all the Yoda moves go to when they die? Noble thought dryly.

Noble followed Abe's Yoda move with an acrobatic move of his own. Noble cleared the opening without jumping or springing, just imagining the movement in his mind.

Great job! Abe said. *Your mind is as nimble as your body,* and then, *Retired Yoda moves indeed. Very funny.*

Suddenly, Abe's eyes were flashing and serious. A wave of killer bugs covered the mountain and ahead of them. Abe started to pound his staff and then stopped with his arm raised in air.

They are sleeping. Abe said. *I see a path that winds around them down the mountain. As long as we are careful not to wake them, it would be better to sneak around them than to draw more attention to ourselves by taking them head on.*

Noble nodded, but as he looked at the path left by the sleeping insects, some with their pincers and stingers raised and snapping, he didn't think he appreciated the idea much.

Eyes open, Noble! Abe said.

You don't have to tell me, Noble said. And then he thought he heard an evil, soft chuckle. But as he strained his ears to listen more closely, it was gone.

Abe and Noble snaked down the path left by the sleeping sentry beetles. They crept at a slow, measured pace, trying not to dislodge small pebbles in their descent. They had to move with care: there was nothing to grab onto to break their fall and nowhere to rest. After what seemed like hours of tip-toeing through dangerous, sleeping bugs, they reached the cave opening. An angry face was carved into the side of the mountain. Its open mouth, a scream, formed the cave opening. Noble and Abe crept cautiously through.

Noble's eyes adjusted to the weaker light. In the cave were shoes, sneakers, a Mickey Mouse shirt, dresses, shirts, and jeans of various sizes. A gleaming object twinkled beneath a worn sneaker. Noble bent to examine it. It was the heart necklace Lark had given Piccolo for Christmas last year. The charm was half of a heart. Lark wore the other half on a chain around her neck. Next to the heart, Noble saw a beaded braid. It looked as if it had been ripped off one's head. Noble thought of the little girl who cried and sang in his dreams: Keisha.

They crept deeper and deeper into the cave. The darkness was thick and black. Noble felt Abe's hand on his shoulder.

Open your mind, Abe said. *See with your mind as well as your eyes.*

Noble focused. He made his way around small rocks and ragged holes in the ground. The air grew hotter and the stench was stronger, more intense. Noble strained, listening closely. Singing, he heard singing and humming.

> This little light of mine
> I'm gonna' to let it shine
> This little light of mine
> I'm gonna' to let it shine –

Noble saw an open pit with a huge fire. A cage of sundry, rotting human and animal bones hung in the air above the pit. From the pit, Noble heard sounds of moaning and gnashing. Inside the cage, Noble saw Piccolo and other small children, Melody, Keisha, and teens from the party the night before. He counted six victims. Noble was relieved that the victims did not seem hurt and that the Darkness had only managed to kidnap six souls, not the needed seven he boasted about in his dreams. Noble made to run toward them, but he immediately stopped and fell back.

Pacing around the burning pit, were the Hell Hounds Glomit and Glut. Lust and Envy in their seductive forms taunted the Innocents in the cage, and standing at the edge of the fire pit was Ba'al.

"I was beginning to worry that I had overestimated you," the mysteriously robed figure said, hissing. It cleaned its nails with the edge of a sharp blade. He pushed the edge of the cage so that it swung back and forth over the fire. The children cried and cringed within.

He looked at the dangerous, leather clad demons and beckoned them closer. "We're being rude," it said. "Why don't we welcome our guests."

Lust and Greed stopped taunting the children in the cage. The children whimpered and clutched each other in fear. They each turned facing Noble and Abe.

Abe and Noble fanned out. Abe held out his staff, and Noble considered the odds of their opponents before them. They were outnumbered over two to one. Abe kept the robed figure in his sight. The hell hounds advanced toward Noble. The twins leaned back against the cave waiting.

"Do you like my babies?" the robed one asked extending his hand to the seductive twins. "They are magnificent. Aren't they?"

"Magnificent?" Abe asked, his eyes were the stormy anger that Noble saw only once before. "Is that what you call monsters that attack innocent children and defenseless victims?"

"Oh, Abram," the robed stranger said. "I should have killed you the first moment I met you, a roving nigger on the road. You never were any fun."

"If what you mean by fun includes killing and maiming, I'd rather remain boring, Ba'al," Abe said.

"And so you shall, Wise One," Ba'al answered. "A bored stiff." He chuckled lamely at his own joke. Noble noticed that he was the only one amused.

The hell hounds moved closer. Noble shook off his bag and stretched out his hands. Heat emanated from his fingertips. He hurled a fire bolt at the closest hound. The blast knocked the hound off its feet. Noble expected the animal to stay down, at least for a few moments. Instead it sprang back to its feet, its skin still smoking from the burn.

"Oh dear!" Ba'al answered. "I think you'll find that Firemight doesn't work here. You'll have to reach into your bag of tricks and try harder. Or is that the only trick you know?" Noble recognized the same chuckle that had haunted his dreams and waking moments. It was him.

The robed being pulled back his hood and laughed louder. Noble saw that his scalp, face, and neck were mottled, scaled, and scarred. A thick, mottled scrap of flesh covered the place where his right eye should have been. The other eye was a glowing, crimson slit. Noble wondered what horrible thing had happened to the demon to cause it to look so deformed. Remaining, ragged tufts of hair sprang from the otherwise, bald, mottled mass. It seemed as if it had survived being burned alive by fire. Even his lips were two, ragged grooves of blackened skin.

Noble looked at Ba'al with unabashed shock and pity.

"Paul," Abe said. "Let the children go. It is over. Let us put behind this cruelty and evil. Let us rest."

"I am no longer Paul!" the scaled being yelled. "Paul died a long time ago when a nigger robbed him of his life and family. My name is Ba'al. And I willingly serve the Darkness."

Both hounds lunged for Noble again. Their sharp, ragged claws and teeth glistened in the light of the fire pit. The twins began tormenting the whimpering children again. The children, Melody, and Piccolo screamed as they swung the cage between them, back and forth over the pit of fire.

Noble tried to summon a weapon, any weapon that could help him defeat the Hellhounds since they were immune to his fire. He kept his eyes on the hounds in front of him and focused.

A large hammer, heavy with the weight of a cool iron appeared in his hands. Noble nearly dropped it as he wrapped both hands around it and swung hard at the first hound. The anvil caught it squarely in the jaw and set its head at a 45 degree angle with its neck. It crashed again onto the floor on its side. This time it did not get up right away. Noble swung again. This time, Noble clipped the other attacking hound on its shoulder and side. Noble heard the crunch of bone and sinew. The hound whimpered and limped back. Noble rested the hammer by his side briefly. He raised it again over his shoulder, poised for another attack.

Again, Noble expected a brief reprieve from the injured beasts. Ba'al waved his hand and mumbled a curse that Noble could not hear. The bent head on the first hound righted itself again on its neck. Noble heard the sound of sinew and bone mending. The Hellhounds sprang to crouching positions, growled fiercely, and lunged. This time, Abe pounded the rocky cave floor with his staff. The loud boom reverberated throughout the cave. Noble could see the traveling sound waves. As soon as the waves reached the beasts and Noble, they froze mid-air like statues. The sound waves kept reverberating and rebounding. When they reached, Ba'al, the twin demons, and the swing cage of Innocents, they froze, too.

Abe spun the staff around in his hand. It became a large, double edged sword. The blade gleamed silver in the firelight.

Ba'al became unfrozen in seconds. He pulled his outstretched hands apart and blew into them. A dust storm emerged from their depths. It spun and grew until there was a mighty sand storm within the cave. Moving clouds of sand assaulted Abe and Noble and blinded Ba'al and his minions from their view.

Noble squinted his eyes. Temporarily handicapped, he could not see an oncoming attack. Abe swung the long, gleaming sword in sharp, sweeping, circles, cutting the air and clearing away the sand. The blades whistled in the air.

Abe had just cleared a small path in front of Noble and himself, when Noble felt a rush of air brush his face as it whizzed by. Two sharp talons flew into the rock behind him. Noble smiled, pleased that the talons had missed them. He looked briefly to his side, thinking to share a moment of triumph with Abe. What he saw caused Noble's heart to skip several beats. Abe stood weakly, bending over his clutched side. Noble followed Abe's stare as Abe looked down at three sharp talons that impaled his stomach and side. Abe grunted and snatched them from his body, throwing them onto the cave floor. Blood oozed from the wounds, blossoming into crimson from Abe's shirt and cloak. He staggered back a few steps and then steeled himself, bracing for another attack.

"Abe!" Noble yelled, dropping the hammer and running to Abe's wounded side.

Not now, Abe projected into Noble's mind. *Focus on the fight!*

"Yes Noble," Ba'al jeered. "Do focus. I need your attention now. We need to talk."

Noble lunged for his hammer but found that one of the hounds had retrieved it, clutching it in his jowls.

"Before you try to stop me or entertain any dreams of saving the day, because you can't, by the way," Ba'al said. "I think you should understand a few things. See reason before it's too late."

"You cannot reason with evil!" Noble spat.

"Oh, dear Abe trained you well," Ba'al said. "I can always recognize a student of his brainwashing. Just make sure you have all of the facts. Both sides of the story."

Noble tried not to look sideways at Abe, feeling his presence, his thoughts, and his injuries in his mind as he positioned himself between Abe and Ba'al. He would not lose him. He tried to quell his anger before it made him lash out irrationally. His mind became cool, collected, and calmly fatal. He feigned interest as he summoned a wall between him and Ba'al. He would not allow him to gain the advantage again. It had nearly cost him Abe.

"Facts?" Noble asked, summoning in his mind all the lessons, all the important facets of information, Abe had patiently taught him. "What facts?"

"That a boy!" Ba'al said. "I knew you could be reasonable. Truly not everyone wants to live the hard way, to believe in all that goody-goody faith and belief mumbo-jumbo. I know. I heard your fears. I listened to your doubts. You need to be sure you're on the right side."

Noble's hands cooled. He cast about in his mind for anything that would help him kill this demon.

"And how is that?" Noble asked, clinching his fists and quelling the flames. An intuition told him that Ba'al fed off of the Light's power, so he would not give him any, not even his Firemight. Noble's hands became too frozen, clinched fists.

"I can't tell what you're thinking," Ba'al said. "Your mind is unreadable, but that's okay. You'll want to hear what I have to say."

"I'm listening," Noble said, keeping his eyes on the movements of the demon twins, the hounds, and most of all Ba'al. He looked with his mind, his whole being, as well as his eyes.

"Careful, careful," Ba'al said. "You need to open your mind to me.

Don't you want to hear about how to heal your mother? Don't you want to bring your father back?"

"Lies," Noble spat. "You don't want to heal my mother or bring my father back. They're too much of a threat. You need to be open, too, Ba'al. What do you really want?" Noble felt the excitement in Abe's mind, once he caught on to the reasoning of Noble's words. He also felt his strength waning, a weakening pulse. He tried to keep his mind focused and the wall up, firmly in place. He would not reveal his hand. Not yet.

"Clever boy!" Ba'al yelled. "That's why I like you. We're more alike than you know. You're right. I could kill your mother. Right now if I wanted to. I just want to help."

Noble remained silent at Ba'al's words. He wanted to take Abe's sword and cleave his head in two, but he kept his emotions and his thoughts firmly concealed behind the wall.

Ba'al waved his hands and a flickering image of his mother's hospital room appeared. It roiled and bristled in the air of the dark cave. His mother groaned, from her position in a fetal ball beneath the covers. Her body shook with pain. An attending nurse hovered over her, checking her pulse, reading her temperature, and flipping through her chart. Instinctively, Noble felt the danger radiating from the nurse. The nurse's eyes glared crimson beneath lowered lids. She placed a pale green hand across his mother's knee. His mother screamed out in pain.

"We're just getting started, Honey," the nurse said in a cruel smile. His mother writhed in agony as the chee-wee-chee-wee chewed its way up her leg, the muscle, bone, and flesh. It ravaged her thighs, knees, and hips.

Noble's mother sat upright from beneath the sheets.

"I command you to leave me alone, evil demon!" Genesis said through clenched teeth.

"I wondered how long it would take you to recognize me. Did you miss me, I mean us?" The nurse's body pulled apart and became two forms instead of two.

"I thought I killed you," Genesis said. "No matter. I'll try harder."

"That's the spirit!" the evil twins crooned. Lust and her brother bowed their heads, in introduction. They spoke with one voice. "We are Minion, for we are many. You didn't think you could actually heal, did you? So naïve. Just like your Son!" They stressed their s sound in their words, sounding like hissing snakes.

Noble looked away from the image to Ba'al.

"I'm confused, Noble said. "I thought you said you wanted to help me. How is this supposed to help me?"

"I said, I could kill her if I wanted to right now, as a matter of fact," Ba'al said. "Unless you give me the Nazarene Tear."

"I don't have it," Noble said. "And even if I did, you only have six victims. You were supposed to seize seven."

"But I do have seven," Ba'al said. "I have you. Now you can watch your mother die, and then violently die---" He gestured with his monstrous, scaly hands, placing one finger up to his temple in mock thought.

"Or you can see her released, not killed, and then submit, willingly," Ba'al said. "The choice is yours."

Noble felt Abe's grief and anger. Noble realized that Ba'al would kill his mother anyway. He just wanted the Nazarene Tear. But why? Why would the Tear be so important to Ba'al. Being a creature of Darkness and evil he could not wield it. And then Noble remembered. Abe had called him Paul, Master Paul, the pitiless slaveholder who had killed Elijah, who had begged evil to get back at him. Elijah had been powerful then, but he was untouchable now. Noble would never deliver Elijah, the gentle boy who asked for his help and suffered so greatly to Ba'al. He reached out to all who loved him as he realized now what he must do: Dad, Lark, Momma, Nick, and Abe. Without revealing his thoughts to Ba'al, he reached out to Abe and thanked him for being the surrogate father who loved him in his father's absence. He brushed the face of his mother, briefly alleviating her pain. He asked the Light and all he knew that was right and good to forgive him his doubts and errors, as he tried to complete his quest. He reached out to Elijah, and thanked him, too. He used all of his mind and powers to summon the double edged sword, Truth. He would use it to kill that bitch demon and his brother and free his mother himself. Finally, he would use it on himself to prevent the sacrifice, bringing down the cave on Ba'al and his hell hounds before he could injure the children and the innocents. He wanted his last images to be of Melody as he released her and the other Innocents.

"I'm waiting," Ba'al said. "You can't be afraid of dying, my spies showed me that you were brave. Where is Elijah?"

There it was, a slip. Ba'al had not asked for the Tear, he asked outright for Elijah, which is what he wanted more than destroying the world. He didn't care. He was petty Master Thomas, after all. Never learning. Noble was never more sure in his decisions. He looked at Ba'al calmly, the blade of Truth in his hand.

"I can't," Noble said. "I don't know how to summon it, the Tear. Abe never taught me how. We never got to that point in our lessons."

"Surely you must have," Master Paul, not Ba'al growled. Frustration and anger burned in his eyes. He lifted Abe up from his slumped position on the floor, pushing Noble aside. Noble saw the smile in his eyes. His body hung in the air like a ragdoll. "How is it you didn't teach him, Wise One? That was the most important lesson of all. It should have been lesson one."

Master Paul's distraction was all that Noble needed. With his mind, he swung Truth in the image of his mother's hospital room. He made criss-crossing sweeps across the forms of Minion. They divided into four, smoldering heaps on the floor. Next, he aimed at the hellhounds in mid lunge. He made quick work of severing the head of the first beast; it fell in a steaming clump at his feet. He reversed and cleaved the other hound in two. Both parts disintegrated into ash on the cave floor. Next he swung the sword at the rope that held the cave of Innocents. He moved the entire cage at a safe distance away from the firepit. He slashed across the connecting skeletal bones to provide them escape.

Master Paul still had Abe in the air. He saw several more crimson blossoms blooming on Abe's shirt where Paul had tried to torture him into revealing the Tear and therefore Elijah. Noble summoned all of his might to bring down a deluge of cleansing water upon the fire pit and Ba'al and himself. The pit of fire howled and hissed, and Paul threw up a meager wall of protection from the flood, before Noble brought the blade to his throat.

Paul screamed, his hair returning to his burned face, and his hands returning to their human form. "NO!!!" he yelled.

But as Noble brought the blade upon his neck a force stopped him. He had just nicked his throat, blood trickling down his shirt and trembling arms, when gentle hands reached out and held him.

"There is no need for that, Noble," Elijah said. "I am here."

When Noble looked around for Abe, he was gone. Elijah stood barefoot in glistening gold robes. A light emanated from within him and all around him.

"Thank you, young Noble," he said. "You have served well. Only someone who acts to sacrifice himself could summon me. Summon us."

Elijah raised his hands and broke the wall that was Paul's meager protection. He pinned him to the floor. He directed his hands to the cage of Innocents, he crushed the cage bars. From the remnants, he formed a bridge across the pit, now filled with freezing water.

"Use your light, Noble," Elijah said, smiling. His gentle eyes shined and twinkled as Abe had shined. In his cherubic face was ancient wisdom and goodness. "Summon them through, Light bearer."

Noble looked down at his hands to see they were glowing, not with flame, but with light, a blinding, bright light, as Abe had glowed in Lady Ash's tree. Elijah placed his gentle hands at Noble's neck and temple. His touch was cool where Abe's was warm. But it still soothed him. It healed all of the scars and bruises and bites he had suffered. As he looked down at his clothes, he saw that they were clean and mended, too. They glowed, not as brightly as Elijah's but bright enough to serve as a beacon in this other-worldly plane. He stood on firm legs and feet and walked across the bridge of bones. Everywhere he stepped, the bridge turned to golden stone. He reached into the cage and brought out each Innocent, one by one. When they saw Noble reaching his hands into the cage to pull them out they shouted with joy! He reached in, and brought out Little Keisha. He kissed her cheek. She hugged him and skipped across the bridge to Elijah. He reached in again and brought out the little boy, James, the first victim. He shook his hand bravely and walked proudly across to Elijah and Keisha. He reached in again and again, until all of the victims were released. He reached in to Piccolo and Melody. They each hugged him tightly and cried. Melody kissed him on his cheek as Piccolo looked over her shoulder in disappointment. He brought them all across. Finally, he used his powers to smash the cage to pieces.

When Noble and the last Innocent had crossed the bridge, Noble smashed that, too, covering the flooded pit beneath it. He turned to Elijah.

"Where is Abe?" he asked.

Elijah smiled. "First things, first," Elijah said. "Well, Paul, you asked for me and I'm here. Paul was a sobbing heap beneath the force that penned him to the floor. "It's time to go, Paul," Elijah said. "Pity you could not have done something better with your life and family. You had so much love, a treasure for any life, but you would not see it."

"Will I see my wife and children now?" he asked, still sobbing. He was still scorched, but not the powerful demon the Darkness had used, but a piteous lump upon the floor.

"I'm afraid not, Paul," Elijah said. "They have gone on to be with their loved ones in the Light."

Paul nodded. He got up on his feet looked down at his feet. He waited calmly for his end. The floor broke apart beneath him and large, scaly arms reached through the flames from below pulled him through below. Paul did not scream or cry. He did not rage or yell. He went silently. Noble watched, feeling a little sorry for the man who never knew love.

When the floor sealed up over him, Elijah turned towards Noble and grabbed his hand. He pulled him down so that Noble could look into his face and listen to him. It was plain to Noble that what Elijah had to say was not meant for everyone.

"This is for you," Elijah said. He placed a smooth, small thorn in his hand. "For your mother. It will not heal her entirely, for her pain allows her to feel the pain of others and the wounds they carry. It will help her to continue to heal others, but it will also make her pain bearable so that she can continue in the Light until she will be healed. She will be healed, Noble, but at a time, appointed by the wisdom of Light. Please tell her she must not fear anymore. Fear almost cost her her life and yours. She is such a mighty mother and healer, the Light loves her and will make her even mightier."

Elijah hugged Noble around his neck. "This is for you," he said, placing the Tear in his hand. Use it to heal Nick and all the hurting Innocents today. Use it to summon Abe. Believe it or not, he will help you in future quests. Your work is not done, Champion, Lightworker, Flamebearer."

Noble raised his eyebrows. He couldn't imagine Mr. Cedarian helping him, but because Elijah, a walking miracle, had told himself, he would believe him.

"The stone that Abe gave you during your first lesson will help to lead you to your father, Noble," Elijah said. "He is not dead but gone from this realm and the earthly one, and he will need you to help him get back through, to get home to his family and his golden bride, Genesis." Elijah smiled again. "There is power in families, Noble. Continue to love yours, your family of blood and your family of friends in the Light.

"And finally, this is for you," Elijah said. He pointed beyond Noble. Noble turned around and saw Abe walking in a brilliant, golden robe much like Elijah's. Noble ran to hug him.

"Abe," Noble said, choking in sobs. "I'm happy for you. Does this mean I won't see you again?" He noticed Abe's new, golden robes did not have the crimson stains of the tattered, old one.

"You will see me again, Noble," Abe said, hugging him tightly, his eyes shining brightly. "We will meet together again as you continue in your quests as Champion, and we will see each other again in the Light." Noble cried a little, but was not despaired by Abe's words. He knew where Abe was going, and he knew he would see him there again.

"Is Elijah your son?" Noble asked. Abe still embraced him and his eyes shone so brightly they almost blinded him in their brilliance.

"In a way, he is my son," Abe said. "Just like in a way you are mine. And in a way, I am his. Elijah and I are like two sides of a coin. He is the infant, and I am the elder. Yet, we are both ancient and new and, now, part of the Light. I was sent to bring him home, yet he had work to do on this plane. Though he was part of the Light, he remained to help the Innocents. I was sent to prepare the Luminaries, but I was sent most specifically for you. And now that I have fulfilled my destiny here on this realm, I go to the Light. I will watch over you, young Lark, and Nick. Don't give up on him. And if you ever need me, you can summon me. Please use the stone I gave you to summon your father. I have told him briefly as we met between realms that you are the great champion. He is so proud of you, Noble. As he knew you would do well. He says to be kind to your mother, and to tell him that he returns to his golden bride soon."

Abe released his embrace from Noble but still held him gently in his eyes. He reached out to Elijah who before grabbing his hand, hugged Noble again as well. They walked hand in hand in to a brilliant beam of light on the cave floor. They boarded a floating light dais and rose like a lighted escalator in the night sky. The roof of the cave was broken when Noble brought down the flood. Noble watched them until they were a bright star in the sky. He turned around and noticed the children standing quietly waiting for him.

Just as Noble walked towards them, a herd of unicorns flew toward them. Midnight led the brilliant herd that flew across the night sky. Each one lighted in front of an Innocent, leaning down while they grabbed each around their neck and pulled up on their backs. Midnight flew down to Noble last and nuzzled his cheek. Noble could not have been happier to see him.

"Thank you Midnight," he said. He expressed his thanks to his sister in her thoughts. She showed him an image of their mother Genesis resting peacefully in the hospital room. She slept next to her on a bunk bed, beaming with happiness over her mother's recovery, and of Noble and Piccolo's return.

18

Midnight's Flight

The return home was a trip Noble would never forget. The cold hair ripped through his hair and whipped his face. He inhaled the cold, thin air as he passed through the wisps of a cloud. He turned to notice the children behind him. The mischievous wind made a halo of the clicking, jangling braids as little Keisha held on for dear life. Piccolo pressed her lips together. She offered him a weak smile, but it was clear to see that she and the others were terrified as much as they were exhilarated. Melody urged her horned steed next to Noble and Midnight. She reached out and grabbed his hand. He grabbed her back.

Noble closed his eyes and drew upon the light within him. Beams escaped from his fingertips, his eyes, and finally it emanated from his very person. His entire body, Midnight, and the sky around them were aglow.

"Ooooooh," Keisha said. Her eyes were stretched and her mouth open in silent wonder.

Piccolo weakened her grip around her unicorn's neck, and the other children seemed less fearful, taking in the night time wonders around them. The stars shined brightly, and the moon cast its pale light against the penetrating darkness that once covered Salvation. As the unicorns slowed in descent, the small town, the winding roads, Route 122, and the majestic Live Oaks all drew closer. Noble sighed in triumph and relief and tapped Midnight gently along her cheek and neck.

"Home," Noble said. "We're safely home."

EPILOGUE

Noble and Lark waited outside Nick's house at their regular place before the bus stop down the road. Noble looked nervously at Lark, who gave him an assuring smile.

Several minutes passed before they saw Nick's form, bobbing down the path. He did not wear the garish makeup and feminine clothes he wore before. Instead, he wore a faded Nike tee shirt and jeans.

"I have something for you, Nick," Noble said. "You do not have to talk to me, but I still consider you my brother, my friend. You do not have to be mine."

Nick stared at Noble with hard, cold eyes.

"What?" he said.

"This," Noble said, wincing from Nick's cold eyes, hurt that he seemed not to care whether Noble had lived or died. He took out the Nazarene Tear and held it to Nick's forehead. The tear pulsated and gleamed.

Nick stared at Noble wide-eyed, surprised by the appearance of the Tear, and the sparkling iridescence it created in spite of the glaring sun. Nick looked at first alarmed and then relieved. The hard set to his jaw and cold stare faded from his face. He stumbled back into Lark's open arms, his eyes streaming with tears and release.

"I have to get back to Gramps," Nick said after a moment. He didn't seem to know that he had just fallen into Lark's eyes or he had been touched by the Tear. But Noble noticed that though he had not offered to join them or give their favorite handshake, the hardness and anger was gone from his voice and his very demeanor was calm, peaceful.

"Oh, I forgot," Noble said. "This is for you. Momma's on a baking spree again since she got out of the hospital. She cut you half of a seven-layer chocolate cake and some chocolate chip, peanut butter cookies."

"Thanks," Nick said, smiling over his shoulder sheepishly. "I'm so glad your Momma's feeling better." And then he bounded back up to the path to the house with the boarded windows, ghosts, and his snoozing, boozing grandfather.

As Noble looked back at Nick, he felt that Nick would be okay, and then maybe they would, too. He grabbed the stone in his pocket, not knowing yet how to use it to contact his father, but happy that he soon would know how. Anyway, he had a date with Melody this afternoon at the movies. Lark and Piccolo were going to catch a ride with their mother to get "mani-pedis".

Have fun, Noble thought. He wanted to hug his mother and tell how much he loved her again, before he left on his date with Melody.

ABOUT THE AUTHOR

Tishia "Tish" Mishe Chevez Dobson was a writer, educator, and woman of deep faith whose life was filled with purpose, generosity, and quiet brilliance.

A native of Livingston, New Jersey, Tish made Savannah her home after earning her degree in mass communication from Savannah State University. Over the course of nearly three decades, she dedicated herself to the art of teaching—guiding students in high schools, colleges, and universities with compassion, encouragement, and wisdom. Her love of language and storytelling was matched only by her devotion to her students and colleagues.

Tish's passion for writing led her to earn an MFA in Creative Writing in 2010. She gravitated toward the genres that sparked imagination and inspired belief—Christian fantasy, science fiction, and stories rooted in faith and transformation. This novel, lovingly completed and published by her family, is a testament to her creative spirit and the spiritual depth she brought to her work.

More than anything, Tish lived her life as a reflection of her beliefs—grounded in grace, guided by scripture, and shaped by her relationship with Christ. She was a proud member of St. Paul CME Church and a dedicated participant in Bible Study Fellowship. Her faith was not something she spoke about casually—it was woven into everything she did.

Tish was a beloved wife, mother, daughter, sister, and friend. She gave freely of herself, and those who knew her carry her light with them. This book is just one of the many gifts she leaves behind.

www.ingramcontent.com/pod-product-compliance
Lightning Source LLC
Chambersburg PA
CBHW030349200626
46808CB00022B/673